DATE DUE   JUL 0 6

GAYLORD			PRINTED IN U.S.A.

About the Author

Laurie Faria Stolarz was raised in Salem, Massachusetts, and educated at Merrimack College in North Andover. She has an MFA in creative writing and a graduate certificate in screenwriting, both from Emerson College in Boston. She currently teaches writing and French, and is working on *Silver Is for Secrets*, the third book in the trilogy that began with *Blue Is for Nightmares*. Visit her Web site at www.lauriestolarz.com.

To Write to the Author

If you wish to contact the author or would like more information about this book, please write to the author in care of Llewellyn Worldwide and we will forward your request. Both the author and publisher appreciate hearing from you and learning of your enjoyment of this book and how it has helped you. Llewellyn Worldwide cannot guarantee that every letter written to the author can be answered, but all will be forwarded. Please write to:

Laurie Faria Stolarz
℅ Llewellyn Worldwide
2143 Wooddale Drive, Dept. 0-7387-0443-1
Woodbury, MN 55125-2989, U.S.A.

Please enclose a self-addressed stamped envelope for reply,
or $1.00 to cover costs. If outside U.S.A., enclose
international postal reply coupon.

Many of Llewellyn's authors have Web sites with additional information and resources. For more information, please visit our Web site at:

http://www.llewellyn.com

White is for Magic

Laurie Faria Stolarz

Llewellyn Publications
Woodbury, Minnesota

FIRST EDITION
Seventh Printing, 2006

Book design by Rebecca Zins
Book editing by Andrew Karre and Rebecca Zins
Developmental editing by Megan C. Atwood

Cover design by Gavin Dayton Duffy
Cover image (candle) © Stockbyte

Library of Congress Cataloging-in-Publication Data
Stolarz, Laurie Faria, 1972–
   White is for magic / Laurie Faria Stolarz.—1st ed.
      p. cm.
   Sequel to: Blue is for nightmares
   Summary: Seventeen-year-old hereditary witch Stacey Brown is having night-
      mares that predict death again, but this time the murderous stalker is after her.
   ISBN 13: 978-0-7387-0443-2
   ISBN 10: 0-7387-0443-1
   [1. Witchcraft—Fiction. 2. Magic—Fiction. 3. Stalking—Fiction. 4. Schools—
      Fiction. 5. Extrasensory perception—Fiction.] I. Title.
   PZ7.S8757Wh 2004
   [Fic]—dc22   2003065916

Llewellyn Publications
A Division of Llewellyn Worldwide, Ltd.
2143 Wooddale Drive, Dept. 0-7387-0443-1
Woodbury, MN 55125-2989, U.S.A.
www.llewellyn.com
Llewellyn is a registered trademark of Llewellyn Worldwide, Ltd.

Printed in the United States of America

Acknowledgments

Many thanks to members of my writers group for whom I am truly grateful: Lara Zeises, Steven Goldman, Tea Benduhn, and Kim Ablon Whitney—I couldn't have written this without your friendship, advice, encouragement, and critiques. I feel truly blessed to be able to work with such talented and amazing individuals.

Also, thanks to the many family members and friends who have been a source of encouragement and support: Mom, Ed, Ryan, Mark, Lee Ann, Neil, Laurie, Delia, MaryKay, Lisa, Jessica, Haig, Sara, Martha, and everyone in the New England Screenwriters Alliance.

A special thanks to Lieutenant Fran Hart of the Burlington, MA, Police Department and Officer Conrad Prosniewski of the Salem, MA, Police Department for answering all my police-related questions. Thanks to Dr. Kathryn Rexrode, MD, for answering my medical questions.

And, finally, thanks to Llewellyn editors Megan Atwood, Andrew Karre, and Becky Zins for such helpful suggestions, endless enthusiasm, and critical comments.

One

It's happening again.

The bile at the back of my throat burns. I swallow it down and wipe my bottom lip. My head feels like it's cracking open, like an archeologist is trapped inside, chipping away at the bones of my skull. I lean back against the cold ceramic wall tiles and try to hold it all together—the puking, the headaches, the nightmares, my sanity.

My world is falling apart.

I stand up from the toilet and stumble over to the mirror. My eyes are red, the skin beneath them a dark, smoky color. I reknot my hair with a rubber band, noticing my chin—wet from puke spooge. I wipe the goo with my fingers as best I can and tuck the stray strands of dark hair behind my ears. What I really need right now is a hot bath, but the knocking in my head is so intense I want nothing more than to just lie down.

After a thorough toothbrushing and several gargles of mouthwash, I stagger my way back through the common area and into the room. Drea and Amber, my roommates, are asleep. I know I could wake them up, that they'd want to know what's going on—especially after last time—but I almost don't even want to know myself. Not tonight, anyway.

I grab a lipstick from Drea's vanity table and the notepad from beside my bed. I flip the notepad open to a fresh sheet and write the letter *M* across it in the dark-red lipstick, trying my best to make it look smudged, messy—the way it did in my nightmare.

I rip the page free of the pad and stuff it into the pocket of my pajamas. Then I lie back on my bed and pull the covers up over my ears to block out Amber's snoring. But I still feel sick, the juices in my stomach churning away, bubbling up like molten lava. There's only one way I'm going to get any rest tonight.

From my spell drawer, a.k.a. the bottom drawer of my dresser, I pull out a stick of incense, a virgin black candle, a razor blade, and some other assorted spell supplies, including a bunch of red grapes courtesy of Drea's mini-fridge. I collect it all inside my terra-cotta pot and stand up to leave. Except my head is throbbing. I sit back down and peek over at Amber and Drea, in their bunkbeds, the light of the waxing moon casting a shadow over Amber on the top bunk. She turns over, but she's still snoring—her mouth arched open, chest heaving, six cherry-red ponytails sticking out from her head. Drea moves her forearm up over her ear in response, her golden-blond hair separated into two perfectly frumpled braids.

I wonder if I should even bother telling them anything. If maybe I'm just overreacting. It's only happened twice now. And Maura's birthday *is* a week from Saturday. So, maybe that's what's causing it. Or maybe I'm just coming down with the flu.

The terra-cotta pot tucked under my arm, I grab a pocket flashlight from the drawer and make my way out of the room and through the common area. The door to the boiler room is just out in the lobby.

I travel down the dusty wooden steps using the slender beam of the flashlight to guide my way. I know I could flip on the light switch, but the sudden blast of artificial light would only make my head pound more. Instead, I try to make peace with the darkness; I try to imagine it like crushed velvet, enveloping my skin, inviting me further down the creaking stairs and into the boiler room.

It smells musty down here, like leaking pipes. I try to focus on my breath, but for some reason I'm feeling a bit disconnected. Maybe it's because I don't feel well. Or maybe it's because it's been a year since my last bout of nightmares, and a part of me is afraid that, this time, I won't be able to stop it.

I take a deep breath and make my way across the cement floor. There isn't much down here—an old and rattling boiler, a rusty water tank, dorm room furniture in need of repair, and lots of copper pipes that travel along the ceiling. But it's a place where I can be alone, where I don't have to worry about being interrupted or waking anyone up.

I set my supplies down on the altar I've set up—an old computer desk with a crack down the middle—and light the stick of incense. I start with the bunch of grapes. I pass it through the incense smoke, making sure it gets fully bathed in the lavender fumes. I continue charging all the ingredients, concentrating on the long, gray swirls that rise up and wash over my skin, focusing on lavender's ability to soothe.

My stomach gurgles impatiently. I dab my finger with a bit of the oil and touch the top end of the virgin black candle. "As above," I say. Then I touch the bottom, "So below." I touch the center, drag my finger upward, and then run it back down, continuing to moisten the candle's length.

When the candle is fully anointed, I hold it around the base and, with the razor, carve Maura's name into the wax surface, my fingers shaking slightly from the mere thought of her.

Of what happened.

Of what this all might mean.

I rotate the candle counterclockwise three times, focusing on the idea of riddance, and carve the words "rest in peace" on the opposite side from her name—so the guilt will die from my conscience once and for all.

I light the candle and watch a few seconds as the inky black wax heats up and begins to pool around the wick. Then I take the slip of paper from my pocket and stare down at the M—M for Maura, for Murder, maybe. I really don't know.

I toss it into the terra-cotta pot and then pluck the grapes from their stems. "Maura, Maura, rest in peace," I whisper. "May your haunting spirit finally cease." I toss the grapes into the pot, mash them down with my thumb, and picture the contents of my stomach churning and mixing as the purpley pulp juice smooshes against the tips of my fingers. I chase the grapes with several splashes of peppermint oil, and then mix it all up with my fingers, the minty, candy-cane scent mingling with the breath of lavender, overpowering the smell of grape juice.

"Maura, Maura, rest at last," I whisper. "You shall not make me repeat the past." I chant the words over and over again, concentrating on the black candle as it begins to burn Maura away. I concentrate on the mint coating my stomach, soaking up the grape.

After meditating on the spell for several minutes, I hold my watch up to the candlelight—it's 4:05. I'll take the candle back to my room and set it by my bed so it has time to burn down completely. I smother what's left of the incense, spoon the mint and grape mixture into a plastic sandwich bag, and collect everything inside the pot. Thankfully, I feel my stomach begin to ease. Maybe now I'll be able to get some sleep.

I grab everything and am just about to make my way back upstairs when I hear a banging noise coming from the corner, by the water tank.

"Hello?" I stand up, the wheels of my broken chair squeaking back against the cement. I aim the flashlight out in front of me, but the beam is too narrow to see much in the darkness. I take a few steps toward the tank, noticing the window just behind it is open a crack.

There's a shifting against the floor, like someone taking a step.

"Hello?" I repeat. "Who's there?" My hands shake. My heart tightens. I try to tell myself that it's probably just someone who forgot her key. Probably someone who decided to sneak in since the resident director locks the door at midnight.

Closer now. The tank is just a few feet away—just out of reach. "Come out NOW!"

"Stacey?" says a male voice from behind the tank. "Is that you?"

My mouth trembles open. I don't know that voice. It's not Chad's voice. Not PJ's, either. It doesn't belong to anyone I recognize.

"Stacey?" he repeats. His shadow on the wall moves toward me. I panic. The flashlight tumbles from my grip, the terra-cotta pot slips from under my arm, and I hear it smash against the floor.

I whirl around and run for the stairs. The sudden motion causes the candle flame to flicker out, leaving me in complete darkness. I can hear him behind me, his feet hitting against the cement floor with each stride.

"Wait!" he shouts. His voice is followed by a clanging sound, like maybe he crashed into something.

I trip up the stairs, my chin smacking down against the wooden step, wax dripping on my fingers and burning my skin. I grapple my way up, on hands and knees, toward the boiler room door, but I can't quite find the knob.

"Don't run away from me, Stacey." His voice is frantic and insistent.

Wrestling up another step, I impale my knee on something sharp. A nail. A splinter maybe. I hear myself whimper. My stomach turns. Bile coats the insides of my mouth. His footsteps are following me up the stairs. I pull my knee back and hear a cracking sound, like wood. I reach up for the doorknob, this time able to wrap my fingers around it.

The knob turns but the door won't open, like something is barring it. Like someone wants to trap me inside.

Two

I twist and turn the knob, pound at the door. "Help!" I shout, over and over again. I pivot as best I can and throw the candle—hard—toward his voice. I hear him cry out.

I try at the doorknob again. This time it opens. It's Amber; she's let me out. I whip the door closed behind us and grab Amber by the arm.

When we get back to the room the lights are on and Drea is sitting up in bed. "Are you guys all right?"

But I'm breathing so hard, my heart pounding like a fist, that I can't answer.

"Stacey's gone completely whacked," Amber says, closing and locking the door behind us. "I found her Nightmare-on-Elm-Streeting in the boiler room. Maybe slasher flicks are not such a nifty idea before bed."

"What are you talking about?" Drea asks.

"A guy," I say, gaining my breath. "There was some guy down there."

"Who? Freddie Krueger?" Amber giggles.

"No," I say. "I'm serious. I don't know who it was. They locked me down there somehow. I was trapped."

"Wait," Drea says. "Start over. What happened?"

"*This* is what trapped you," Amber says. She plucks a big fat pencil from her pajama pocket. "It was wedged underneath the door. Probably got kicked there by accident."

"I'm gonna call Keegan," I say.

Keegan is the resident director in charge of our dorm. She's basically this granola-and-yogurt-eating, Birkenstock-wearing throwback from the sixties, complete with yoga mat and tie-dye apparel. But she is a *huge* improvement over Madame Discharge, the resident director for the underclasswomen dorms.

I pick up the phone, but Amber nabs it and clicks it off before I can dial.

"You're not gonna go all schoolmarm on us, are you?" She holds the phone behind her back.

"What's that supposed to mean?"

"Think about it." Amber twirls one of her mini-pony-tails in thought. "It was probably just somebody's juicey downstairs—you know, sneaking in for some cuddle. Wouldn't you be upset if Chad was sneaking in to ladle with you, and someone ratted him out?"

"Don't you mean spoon?" Drea asks.

"Not the way I do it." Amber arches her eyebrows up and down.

"Give me the phone NOW!" I insist.

"Why are you being all wiggy? The boiler room is where everybody sneaks in—guys, guests after midnight, people carrying curious liquids," Amber smiles. "Why ruin everybody's fun by finking to the RD?"

"Maybe I just don't think people should be sneaking in," I say. "Or locking people down in a basement."

"Are you kidding?" Amber says. "One of the benefits of the senior houses is that people *can* sneak in. Plus, you were *penciled* in, not *locked* in. And it was purely an accident."

"He didn't try to attack you or anything, did he?" Drea interrupts. "Wait—what happened to your knee?"

I look down. My pajamas are ripped; there's a giant splinter sticking out through the belly of one of the gingerbread-cookie men patterned across the flannel fabric. But my fingers hurt just as much; there are bits of wax caked to the skin. I break one of the leaves off the aloe plant by the window. The clear, syrupy goo oozes from inside the thick, green plant flesh; I apply the goo to the hardened wax droplets to help soothe the burn.

"What the hell happened to you?" Drea moves toward the edge of the bed, her perfectly toned, tanning-bed legs sticking out from a school T-shirt, the giant Hillcrest letters stretched across her chest. She stares at my waxy fingers.

"Candle wax," I say. "My candle blew out when I started running."

"You know, Stacey," Amber begins, "your primitive living thing does have its charm, but modern electricity is way cooler."

Amber's sarcasm spares me the trouble of explaining my knee.

"Maybe we should call someone to look around a bit," Drea says. "Just to be sure."

Amber tosses me the phone. "Go ahead if you want, but it was probably just some prank. You know, some Michael-Meyers wannabe, inspired by tonight's horror movie marathon. I don't know what Student Activities was thinking, especially considering we're coming up on the one-year anniversary. Case in point." Amber pulls an envelope from the pocket of her pajamas. It has my name, Stacey Brown, written across the front.

"Not again." Drea rolls her eyes and sinks back in her bed.

"Someone slid it under our door tonight," Amber says, tearing at the seal. "One of the ghost groupies, no doubt." She unfolds the paper and reads the message aloud: "Five days till death."

"Great," I say.

"Oh, and someone's drawn a cute little knife here beside your name." Amber flashes me the ink sketch.

"How is a knife cute?" Drea asks.

"It has a curly handle." Amber points out the stylish detail. "See what I mean? This stupid school is full of immature urchins with nothing better to do."

It's true we've had our share of pranks this year—phone calls, "I'M WATCHING YOU!" notes stuffed in our mailboxes, the occasional hockey mask or pool of ketchup blood left outside our door or window. All because of last year.

Last year, I was having nightmares—nightmares that turned out to be premonitions, forewarning me that Drea was going to be killed. And then all this stuff started happening. Drea was getting these weird phone calls from some guy who wouldn't tell her his name. And then she started getting these notes and packages, telling her he was coming for her. In the end we were able to save Drea from Donovan, a guy she had known since the third grade, a guy we all knew as the one who would be crushing on her until the day he died. Of course, he wasn't the one who ended up dead.

That was Veronica Leeman.

.　.　.

Despite Amber's efforts to convince me that the incident down in the boiler room was just another prank, I call Keegan anyway and tell her everything that happened, including the part about the window being open a crack but minus the part about the spell. She tells me that she'll check it out and get back to me. I know there's a chance that Amber might be right, but I honestly don't feel that she is. Why else would I be feeling this enormous sense of déjà vu?

I rub the aloe gel into the burn and, with my other hand, assess the damage to my knee. It's not as bad as it feels. I can see the splinter piece through the skin on my kneecap—a good sign. I grip the part sticking out and pull, watching the splinter move its way toward the puncture spot.

Amber grabs her wallet off the night table and hands it to me. "Here, gnaw down on Scooby. That's what I do when I have to pluck my eyebrows." She feeds the wallet into my mouth before I can object.

"From what I can see," Drea runs a finger over one of Amber's eyebrows, "it looks like Scooby hasn't been nibbled in a while."

"Maybe not," Amber says, feeling between her eyebrows for fuzz. "But at least *he* gets some tongue action."

"What's *that* supposed to mean?"

"If the nun habit fits . . ." Amber flops down atop my bed, knees bent, feet facing in toward one another, making the Porky Pigs of her slippers kiss.

I ignore them as best I can and resume my splinter plucking, trying to keep my hand steady so it comes out in one piece. Despite excess drool, the wallet actually helps, and, with only a few grunts, I'm able to pull the splinter out.

Except there's still some dirt left under my skin. I pull a fresh lemon from my spell drawer and cut it in half with a plastic knife. Like my grandmother, who basically taught me everything I know about the art of kitchen witchery, I always keep a healthy supply of spell items on hand. You just never know when you'll need them. Like last week when Drea asked me to help her make a luck sachet for an English exam. Or the week before that when I whipped up a batch of moon soap for Amber's PMS.

My grandmother always used lemons for cuts. She would squeeze the fruit of its juice, allowing the juice to drain into a bowl, add a teaspoon of vanilla extract, mix it up, and then apply the mixture to the wound. I make an attempt to do the same, but it seems I've run out of vanilla. Weird—I could have sworn I still had a full bottle. I dip a rag into the lemon juice anyway and apply it to the wound, hoping it will suffice.

The phone rings a few minutes later. It's Keegan. She tells me she checked out the boiler room and aside from the open window—which she has since closed and locked—everything looks clear, except, she adds, for a broken pot of some sort and a weird candle left behind. I thank her and hang up, feeling somewhat relieved but still uneasy.

"Keegan said everything looks okay," I say.

"What were you even doing down there?" Drea asks.

But I don't feel like explaining my Maura spell. "I just thought I heard something."

I hate having to lie to them, especially after everything they've been through with me. But I just don't want to say anything yet. I have no idea why Maura is, once again, haunting my nightmares. I thought I had closed the book on that. I thought I forgave myself for everything that happened. But maybe I haven't. Maybe somewhere deep inside me there's this rotting place of guilt. Maybe that's why I've been throwing up.

Three

While Amber and Drea fall back asleep, I lie awake and stare up at the ceiling. There's really no point in sleeping since I didn't get to finish my spell. No point in having to wake up again to a mouth full of puke. Especially since I only have another few hours before I'd get up anyway.

Instead, I try my hardest to focus on Maura, the little girl I used to babysit. I try to figure out why I'm dreaming about her again, why my subconscious mind is stirring up old ghosts.

When I feel my mind begin to wander and my eyes start to get heavy, I turn to glance at the clock by my bed. It's almost six. I think about calling Chad, but I know he'd still be asleep. And I honestly don't know what I'd say to him, if I'd even tell him about tonight. I feel bad I didn't call him back last night, like I was supposed to. But lately I feel as though I've been pushing him away. I think it's because of Drea. I mean, I love Drea like a sister, and I'm so glad she decided to come back to Hillcrest for our senior year. But it's just so weird, me dating her ex-boyfriend and all.

When Chad and I first started going out, just after Donovan's murder trial ended and Donovan was sent away, it was easier. Drea wasn't around. She ended up going home for the remainder of our junior year to try to put the pieces of her life back together. And it's not as though I wish she'd stayed away. It was just easier before she came back. I mean, I know she gave us her blessing; I know she says it doesn't bother her, but I can't help feeling that she's still in love with him. And even if she isn't, I feel like I'm breaking some sort of unwritten rule about not dating your best friend's ex.

The cut on my knee is stinging. I wonder if it's because I didn't have that vanilla extract. I consider searching the common-room pantry; maybe there's a bottle stashed away in one of the cupboards. But then I remember my own stash—in the overnight bag my mother bought me four years ago, when I first got accepted to Hillcrest. I sometimes toss various spell supplies in there, usually stuff that doesn't get used that much— random trinkets and ingredients I come across that I think I might use later, like that container of onion powder I bought on sale or the leaf-shaped seashell I found on the beach one summer.

I pull the bag from the back of my closet, unzip it, and stare down at the contents. Lying practically on top is the full bottle of vanilla extract I knew I had. The onion powder and seashell are still in there as well. And so is the thick white candle my grandmother gave me on my twelfth birthday, just a couple months before she passed away. I had completely forgotten about it.

It's one of the hand-poured kinds, about ten inches tall and as thick as my fist. I still remember my grandmother giving it to me. It was nighttime, after my friends had left, after all the other birthday presents had been put away. Gram and I sat on her back porch under the blanket of the dark sky, just the swollen moon above us. She set the shimmery silver package on my lap. "Open it with care," she said.

I remember unwinding the crinkly paper and marveling at the brightness of the candle wax against my skin. A virgin candle, never used, with a clean, white wick.

"A white one?" I smiled.

"White is for magic," she explained. "You should only use white candles for the most magical of occasions and you should only light this one when you feel the time is right."

"When will that be?" I asked, sniffing at the wax, hoping for the scent of coconut or vanilla bean.

"When you feel in your heart the truest, most meaningful aspect of magic."

"What *is* the truest, most meaningful aspect of magic?" I asked, disappointed in the candle's lack of scent.

She smiled, her cheeks pinkening over. "It isn't my place to tell you. One day you'll know. You'll feel it."

"Can't you just tell me, Gram?" I moaned.

She shook her head. "If I told you, you'd only know it in your mind, not in your heart. There's a big difference."

Of course, at twelve years old, I had absolutely no idea what she meant. I *still* don't. But, even though I obviously never did light this white candle, I *have* used white candles before—whenever I've wanted to cause magical things to happen, whenever I felt a spell or remedy needed that extra magical touch.

The problem is I know such occasions are not what she was referring to. I grip the candle in my palm and hold it up to my cheek, remembering my grandmother's soft, smooth skin, the way her voice got all whispery when she told me all this.

Instead of returning the candle to the bag, I decide to keep it out. I set it atop my night table, concoct a fresh batch of the lemon–vanilla-extract mixture, and apply the ointment to my wound. Already it feels better.

Now what?

Since I don't have one of those book-light things, I grab the phone and my English reader and make my way out to the common room, where I know I won't wake anyone up. Maybe I'll wait until seven and then give Chad a call. I plunk myself down in the lime-green easy chair in the corner, in lieu of one of the straight-back, studious ones—a major mistake since I'm itching for sleep. The soft, velvety corduroy cushions cuddle me up like a favorite sweater. I click the lamp on and flip open to the Raymond Carver story I'm supposed to have read by B-block today.

I'm just about to start skimming over the post-reading section when I hear a clomping sound, like footsteps, coming from out in the lobby. I get up from the chair and walk slowly toward the sound. It's coming from behind the boiler room door, like someone's coming up the stairs. I take a deep breath and silently count to ten, telling myself that it's probably some girl who forgot her key. But then I hear voices—male voices—whispering, talking back and forth.

I grab an umbrella from the collection by the entrance and position myself next to the boiler room door. I know I'm acting like some paranoid freak, that it's probably just like Amber said—probably some girl's boyfriend trying to sneak in after curfew. It's just that the idea of someone breaking in, of sneaking around at this hour, time-travels me right back to the past. When I had legitimate reasons to be a paranoid freak.

I raise the umbrella high above my head and watch as the knob turns and the door edges open.

It's Chad.

"What are you doing?" I drop the umbrella and smack my hand over my heart. "How did you get in here?"

The door swings open completely. PJ's there, too. He's holding a twisted-up bobby pin between two fingers.

"I knew *he'd* be able to get us in," Chad says.

"Hey, Love Dove." PJ air-kisses me on both cheeks. "Getting into the basement was a piece of cake, but the main door? Forget about it."

"So how *did* you get in? The window downstairs?" I thought Keegan said she locked it.

"Can't let the ol' kitty cat out of the Sak's bag completely," PJ says. "These lips are sealed." He twists his lips locked.

"You weren't down there earlier, were you?"

"Who wants to know?" PJ asks, puckering up at me.

"We just got here a few minutes ago," Chad says. "Calm down. What's the big deal?"

"The big deal is that people shouldn't be allowed to just break into campus buildings whenever they feel like it. How were you guys even able to make it over here from your dorm? Isn't campus police doing their job?"

"Puh-*leeze*," PJ says. "When the Dunkies shuts down at midnight, so do they."

"Relax." Chad rubs my back to soothe me. "You're gonna wake everybody up."

"It's just way too easy for people to sneak into this place. You'd think at a prep school dorm there'd be a lot more . . . safety."

"I've got some safety right here." PJ rustles in his jacket pocket.

"Look," Chad begins, "I'm sorry we scared you. I wasn't thinking. *Obviously* I wasn't thinking. I just wanted to see you." He pries the umbrella from my fingers and deposits it in the holder by the entrance.

"I think I'm going crazy," I say.

"Crazy for me, I hope." He smiles and wraps me up in his arms. And he smells so good, like cinnamon mixed in hot apple cider, making it way too difficult to sustain anger. I run my fingers though his sandy-blond hair and burrow my nose into the collar of his jacket.

"I think I'm gonna puke," PJ says. "This is way too sweet tart for me. Where's *my* squeeze?" PJ thumps his hand over his heart, enabling me to catch a glimpse of the tiny lady-bugs he's got painted across his black-polished fingernails.

"She's not exactly your squeeze anymore," I say, breaking the embrace.

"Don't let her snooty, standoffish routine pull the fleece over your eyes, little one. The girl absolutely gummies me." PJ runs his palm over the three-inch plum-purple spikes of his hair and then saunters off to prey on Amber in our room.

Meanwhile, Chad and I move into the common area and squeeze into the cushy love seat.

"You shouldn't be here, you know," I say. "We're gonna get suspended."

"Only if we get caught." He nuzzles his forehead against mine, making me almost forget that Keegan's door is just down the hall. It's just that he looks so good. His greeny-blue eyes are framed by wire-rimmed glasses. A cuddly cotton sweatshirt fits snugly across his chest. An off-center smile curls up to the left.

"What are you even doing up?" I ask.

"Drea called me."

"She *did?* When?"

"Yeah," he says. "A little while ago. It's no big deal. She was just calling to ask me a question about the pre-calc test we're having today, and then she told me how you got spooked earlier—something about someone scaring you in the boiler room? . . . Anyway, I thought I'd just come by to check on you—surprise you. Is that okay?"

I feign a nod, even though I hate surprises. Even though it irks me that he hasn't figured this out yet. And what's worse is the idea that Drea called him in the first place— that as soon as I step out of the room she decides to go behind my back with some bogus excuse about studying for a test. The girl hasn't opened a book since before dinner last night, for god's sake.

"I'm sorry," he says.

"It's okay," I say, taking a deep breath, reminding myself that it's a brand new year.

Chad leans me into his chest and kisses the top of my head. "You need to relax. It's safe here. Everything's gonna be fine."

"I know," I say, biting my lower lip.

"Donovan's gone. It's time to let it go."

"This has nothing to do with Donovan," I say, sitting up.

"I think it might."

"And *I* think you're missing the point."

The door to our room opens. It's Drea, her paisley-printed pillow clutched under her arm and her comforter trailing out behind her.

"Oh, sorry," she says. "Did I interrupt something? I was just gonna sleep out here. Amber and PJ won't stop arguing."

"Sorry we woke you," Chad says. "PJ and I should probably get going anyway. I just wanted to check on your roommate here—surprise her with a little after-hours visit."

"That's *so* sweet," Drea squeals.

"*I* thought so," he says. "Anyway, I don't want you guys to get in trouble."

"No," Drea says. "It's fine. I'll just sleep out in the lobby." She lets out a long-winded sigh and then makes her way in that direction, her perfect pout matching her even more perfect Victoria's Secret supermodel legs, making me want to shove her out the door completely. I know she knows what she's doing. And I also know it's no mistake that she came out here dressed like *that*.

"I'll call you later." Chad kisses my cheek granny-style before nabbing PJ from our room.

"Ciao for now, my little brown cow," PJ says to me. "And, next time, ix-nay on the scary oovies-may."

"Huh?"

"The scary movies . . ." he clarifies, a hint of annoyance in his voice. "Just say no." He hums a few notes from the theme song to *Halloween*, blows me a kiss, and then makes his exit with Chad.

"Well, I guess I can go back to bed now," Drea says. She smiles at me, making me almost want to pick out her teeth one by one. But since my fuming is still focused on

Chad—and on campus security's inability to do its job after everything that's happened at this stupid campus—I decide to spare her and, instead, check out the window in the boiler room for myself.

four

The door to the boiler room is open a crack—most likely from Chad and PJ's visit. I leave it open completely and click on the stairwell light. The sudden burst from the light-bulb, dangling just overhead, stings my eyes and causes my head to start throbbing again. I make my way down the creaky stairs, telling myself that I'm not afraid, that if the window is open, I'll simply close it and lock it back up.

I reach the bottom of the stairs and take a deep breath. That's when I sense it, when I feel it. Something isn't right. I reach for the pull chain overhead and tug it firmly to click on the lights. The long and narrow fluorescent strips glare down from the unfinished ceiling, lighting the entire boiler room.

The back of my neck turns cold and a chill runs down my shoulders. I look around, in all corners of the room, to be sure I'm alone. There are several desks stacked up against the wall. I move closer, trying to angle my glance to see if someone might be hiding behind them. I ball my hands into fists in an effort to prepare myself for the worst. But it's just empty behind there—no one. I let out a breath, loosening the binds in my chest, and move toward the water tank—toward the window.

As I get closer, I can feel a coolness, a subtle breeze that pats along my arms and over my shoulders. It's the breeze filtering in through the window crack. I move behind the water tank and feel my entire body freeze over. The open window is in full view now. But even more alarming is what's painted across it—the letter *M*, crudely splattered against the glass in a dark-red color. Just like in my nightmare.

I feel the door in my heart slam closed, but quickly realize that it's really the door upstairs, the one I entered, the one to the boiler room. And that the stairwell light has been clicked off. I steel myself in place and silently count to ten, mentally preparing myself for what comes next. After several seconds I feel myself take a few steps backward, just staring at the *M*, fearing I know exactly what it means.

Somehow I'm able to turn away from it, to grab hold of myself and scurry as fast as I can up the stairs, tripping up a couple steps along the way. I fling the door open, hear it bang against the wall, and I run back to the room, slamming and locking the door shut behind me.

"What's going on?" Drea clicks on the light beside her bed.

"Something's happening." My body is trembling all over. I cross my arms in an effort to stop the quake.

"Stace, you're as pale as my ass," Amber says. "What happened?"

"Downstairs," I choke. "On the window—the letter *M.*"

"*What?*" Amber asks.

"*M?*" Drea sits up and moves to the edge of her bed.

I nod.

"*M-what?*" Amber asks. "What are you talking about?"

"*M,*" I say, my voice rising up. "For Maura. For *Murder.*"

"What?" Drea gasps.

"Why were you down in the boiler room again?" Amber asks.

"Aren't you listening to me?" I grab at the ache in my head.

"Wait," Drea says. She springs from her bed and stands in front of me. "Go slower. Start from the beginning."

"Just come down to the boiler room with me. See for yourself."

Drea wraps an arm around my shoulder and a whimper escapes from my throat. Amber hops out of bed as well and joins us on our trip downstairs.

I flick the stairwell light back on—the lights in the downstairs part are still on—and lead Drea and Amber across the cement floor and behind the water tank. And I almost can't believe what I'm seeing—or not seeing. The *M* is gone.

"The window," I whisper.

"Yeah?" Amber snaps. "You're right, there *is* a window there."

"No," I say, staring at the clear glass.

Amber runs her hands over the window and checks the lock. "It's even locked . . . imagine that." She turns around to face me.

"No," I say. "It was there—the letter *M*. And the window was open a crack."

"Are you sure?" Drea asks. She rests her hands on my shoulders, in an effort to calm me, maybe—to look into my eyes and understand.

I nod, my jaw trembling slightly. It just doesn't make sense.

"And so what if it *was* there?" Amber says. "It's probably been there for months."

"No," I say, taking a step closer to the window. "I would have noticed it before."

"What difference does it make," she says. "It's gone now and, in case you've forgotten, *your* name starts with an *S*."

"You don't understand."

"Well, then, make me understand—because right now I'm starting to think you're completely funkified."

I look to Drea. I can see she wants to believe me, and maybe a part of her already does.

"Forget it," I say, maybe as much for my sake as for hers. I'm not sure she could handle what's been going on inside my head, what I feel in my heart might be happening again—not after last year. "Maybe I just need some sleep."

"*That's it?*" Amber's face drops. "What about 'M for Maura? M for Murder?' Have you completely wigged on us?"

"I'm sorry," I say, even though I know the M was there, that it was real. That my nightmare predicted it. I take one last look at the window before turning away to go back upstairs.

five

My day goes by in an absolute blur. After a night packed with enough chaos and conflict to fill up an entire season of daytime drama, my classes seem almost incidental. I mean, how am I supposed to focus on French and astronomy when everything seems to be crumbling to pieces all around me? And yet, if I don't start buckling down, the chances of me getting into a halfway-decent college will be slim to none.

That's why I've decided to make an actual attempt at studying tonight. That *and* because I've managed to find myself sleepless once again. It's not that I *can't* sleep; I just don't want to. Every time I feel myself nodding off, I get that sour feeling in the pit of my stomach, like I'm going to be sick. So, while Drea and Amber snooze soundly in their beds, I sit out here in the common room, pounding away at my bio notes, hoping the words in bold will somehow cosmically soak into my brain.

Except I can't stop thinking about last night.

My grandmother's white candle resting in my lap, I close my eyes and picture the letter *M*—red and splattered—the way it appeared against the window glass. I realize that someone could have been playing yet another stupid prank, or maybe it was meant for someone else—some sort of private joke that has absolutely nothing to do with me. Or, per Amber's theory, maybe I really *was* funkified. It's true I was beyond the point of exhaustion last night—or, should I say, the wee hours of this morning. I could have imagined the whole thing. And I know I sometimes dream about things that have little or no relevance to real life.

But I know in my heart none of that is true. I know that marking was there—I felt it; I saw it.

And I know it was meant for me.

I bring the candle up to my nose and whisper the letter *M* over and over again, hoping the magical elements of the whiteness will help lead me in the right direction. It feels good just holding the candle, having it close to me—its mystery, its mysticism. Almost as if my coming across it so suddenly was my grandmother's way of showing or telling me something.

I reach into my pencil case for a red marker and dip the tip into my mug of water. The red ink begins to filter across the surface in puffy, cloudlike shapes, turning the water a slight pinkish color. I move into the pantry and stand in front of the sink. The window above the faucet is similar to the one downstairs in the boiler room. I draw a giant *M* across it, trying my best to make it look messy, the way it appeared downstairs. The water helps, causing the bright red lines to bleed down the glass. I stare at it—hard—trying my best to concentrate, hoping the duplication will promote some sort of insight. And still, the words that flash across my mind are the ones I fear the most: "Maura" and "Murder."

I feel my chin quiver. I grab a paper towel to wipe up my mess. The marker lifts quite easily, leaving the glass completely clear. All except for a face—reflecting right at me. I gasp and turn around.

It's Drea.

"Couldn't sleep?" she asks.

I let out my breath. "You scared me."

"Sorry," she says. "What are you doing?"

"Studying."

"Really?" She scrunches up her lips. "Kind of hard to study when you're washing windows."

I look down at the paper towel in my hand, splotched with red, and crumple it up so she doesn't see the stain. "You're right. I couldn't sleep." Not a total lie, after all.

"Oh?" Her face crinkles up in confusion. "I thought that maybe you might be out here talking to Chad."

"And what if I was?"

"Nothing," she says, twirling a lock of blond around her French-manicured fingernail. "I just had a homework question to ask him. No big deal."

I nod, even though I know she's completely lying. "After my not-so-tickled reaction to his visit last night," I say, "I'm pretty sure it'll be a while before he makes another unannounced appearance."

"He isn't mad at you, is he?" Drea asks, probing further.

I shrug, even though I noticed he was definitely distant with me today. It was just after hockey practice when I saw him and he was still with his teammates. But he was all, "Hey, what's up? I'll talk to you later." Like he was talking to any other girl. And I'm *not* just any other girl. I'm the girl*friend*.

"I need to study," I say, choosing not to discuss this with Drea, of all people.

She takes the hint and turns on a bare heel to go back into the room. Meanwhile, I fill the kettle with water from the tap and set it on the stove for a cup of tea. Maybe a dose of caffeine will help me focus better, help me to get some studying done once and for all.

I flop back into the lazy chair and make an effort to read over the stuff I've highlighted, but I'm so completely tired. I lay my head back against the cushion and close my eyes, imagining thick and velvety rose petals lying over my eyelids, imagining myself slipping into a steamy-hot bath sprinkled with chamomile petals while lavender incense smokes and the sound of rain comes down from outside.

The door to the hallway bathroom slams shut, snapping me back to reality. I wonder who else is up at this hour. I peek toward the hallway, at the rooms on the opposite side of the common area, but the doors are closed.

I shake away the urge to snooze and resume my reading, trying to predict which questions Mr. Milano will ask during his discussion, wondering if he'll give us another pop quiz. I hear the shower valves squeak on. I turn a page to peruse the review questions at the end of the chapter, and then I hear something else. A loud cracking sound coming from the bathroom, followed by a giant thud.

The hum of the water hitting against the shower floor continues. I reposition myself in the chair and make an effort to resume my work, but I can't concentrate, not until I know for sure everything's okay. I flip my book closed and creep across the wooden floor toward the bathroom. The bathroom light doesn't even look like it's on. The crack at the bottom of the door is dark.

I press my ear up to the door, but I don't hear anything—just the water as it showers down from the nozzle. Concentrating on the sound, I notice that the stream of water sounds odd as it hits the tile floor, as though nothing interrupts its path.

As though no one's even in there.

I knock. No response. I knock again. "Hello? Who's in there?"

Still no response.

I try the door. It's locked.

I stand there a few moments, trying to figure out what to do. I suppose I could have Amber pick the lock, since she's good at that. Or I could bother Keegan again and ask for help. I knock a few more times, trying to concentrate on the image inside, trying to picture one of the girls brushing her hair or shaving her legs. But I just can't; my mind's eye can't see anyone in there.

I hurry back into the pantry, pull a fondue fork from the utensil drawer, and then stick it into the bathroom lock. I jiggle it back and forth, listening to the prongs as they scratch against the metal interior. The whistle of the teapot screams from the stove. I just need another minute. I continue to maneuver the fork in the lock for several seconds until I'm able to nuzzle the tip into a crevice. I turn it. *Click.*

Shaking now, I place my hand around the knob, turn the light switch on, and push the door wide open.

It's Veronica Leeman.

Veronica Leeman, who died last year.

Her body is sprawled out on the floor, just like it had been the night I found her. Blood, running from her head where Donovan hit her. Her deep, moss-green eyes stare right up at me, disappointed that I couldn't save her.

My breath quickens, puffing out my mouth. Glass breaks in my chest. I don't know if I'm going to cry or be sick. Instead I hear myself scream—a long, piercing squeal that burns out my throat.

The scream wakes me up out of sound sleep. Out of another nightmare.

It takes a few seconds for reality to check in. I'm still in the common room, still sitting in the same lime-green comfy corduroy chair, my biology notebook opened up on my chest, the white candle sitting in my lap.

Doors swing open all around me. Girls on the floor rush from their rooms to see if I'm okay, to see what happened. They're standing all around me, asking me all sorts of questions—their lips moving, cheeks puffing, hands on hips, eyebrows moving up and down.

But I don't hear them. Because I'm still shaking. Still paralyzed by what I saw. It was just so real. Veronica Leeman's eyes.

One girl—Trish Cabone, I think—goes to the stove and silences the screaming kettle. Keegan kneels down in front of me. She looks at her watch, rubs my forearm, and then mouths some words, but all I can do is look to Drea and Amber, who push their way through everyone. It appears as though Drea is giving some explanation. And then Amber tails it with something funny; I can tell from the way she's getting everyone to laugh.

Drea takes my hand and leads me out through the crowd, back into the room, all the while moving her mouth wide as though shouting out over all their voices. They close the door, and then she and Amber tuck me back into bed, each taking a place beside me while I burrow myself into the covers and picture Veronica's eyes.

Six

I sleep through B-block English—dreamlessly, thankfully. When I wake up, I have to blink a few times to focus, my eyes adjusting to the blurs of navy blue and green plaid atop my bed—Drea and Amber, sitting on each side of me, already suited up in their school uniforms.

"Are you okay?" Drea asks.

"Why aren't you guys in class?" I ask, sitting up.

"You're not exactly in class yourself." Amber fluffs the giant purple flower she's got pinned in her hair.

"I called the school counselor and told her you were having a little . . . trauma." Drea clears her throat.

"You did *what*?" I ask.

"It was the only way all three of us could get away with skipping class. We're supposed to be comforting you."

"Yeah," Amber says. "So you better freakin' let us."

"And then you can let Mrs. Halligan," Drea says, squaring the tip of her nail with a file. "She's expecting you on her happy sofa as soon as you can make it."

"Great," I sigh. "I suppose I have nothing better to do than waste time talking to the school shrink."

"So, what's going on?" Drea asks.

I glance toward my night table, noticing the white candle sitting atop my biology textbook. Drea or Amber must have retrieved them for me. "I had a nightmare," I say.

"Yeah," Amber twists a ponytail around her finger, "we sort of had that part figured out. The blood-curdling screams were a dead giveaway. The hard part was trying to explain to everyone that that kind of behavior is normal for you."

"How *did* you explain?"

"No Homework Excuse #105."

"Which is?"

"Serious bout of the hemorrhoids."

"Oh my god," I say. "Tell me you're joking."

"No joke," Amber says. She grabs her pair of square black eyeglasses, scoots them down toward the tip of her nose, and snatches Drea's nail file. She files away at her sparkly purple fingernails.

"She's lying," Drea says. "It actually wasn't that hard to explain. I mean, after last year."

"Yeah," Amber says. "It's almost like people expect that kind of psycho behavior from you. I know *I* do."

I wince at the word, at the thought of myself labeled like some Hitchcock movie. But what's worse is that she's right.

"What was your nightmare about?" Drea asks.

I take a deep breath and exhale for five full beats. There's really no point in holding off telling them any longer. And so I just say it. "Veronica Leeman." Her name sounds so surreal on my tongue—like some unspoken secret buried deep in the ground where no one can touch it.

"Veronica?" Drea's steel-blue eyes widen. "Why were you dreaming about *her*?"

"Because she's dead. And maybe I'm the one responsible."

Drea's mouth quivers into a frown. I'm not sure I should even be talking about any of this with her. Maybe she isn't ready to hear that I'm having nightmares again. I'm barely even ready myself.

"Not this again." Amber stands up and picks a three-finger wedge from her tights. "We tried to save Veronica. We did everything we could have."

"You don't really believe you're responsible, do you?" Drea asks.

I shrug. "I'm not sure about anything anymore. I mean, I know I tried my hardest. I know I did my best to read my nightmares, my premonitions. It's just . . . I have no other explanation as to why I'm dreaming about old ghosts."

"Wait," Drea says. "What are you talking about?"

"I'm having nightmares about Maura too," I say. "I mean, it's only happened a few times, but they're the same nightmares I had right before she was kidnapped. Right before she was killed."

It's weird to be talking about Maura again. When I was able to save Drea from Donovan last year, I felt that in some small way I was putting Maura's memory to rest—like I could finally forgive myself for ignoring the recurring nightmares I had about Maura three years before, for ignoring the premonitions that might have saved her life. But now I'm having my doubts.

I close my eyes and think of that watercolor picture Maura made for me, painted with eight-year-old hands— the two of us on her porch swing. It's tucked away in my scrapbook, but I suddenly have the urge to go and take it back out; I just miss her so much.

"Wait," Amber says. "Does this have anything to do with last night—the whole 'M for Maura' business?"

"It could," I say. "I saw the letter M in my nightmare, too. Not on a window. More like pressed behind my eyes."

"So, what does that mean?" Amber asks.

"I honestly don't know."

"Why does it have to mean anything?" Drea asks. "So you dreamt about an M and then saw it in reality. You've dreamt about lots of pointless little details before—like that dream you had about fuzzy yellow socks and then Amber showed up wearing a pair. This could be the same sort of thing. It doesn't mean something bad is going to happen."

"I guess," I say, fully understanding Drea's need to try and make light of the situation.

"But then why are you having nightmares about dead people?" Amber asks.

"Your guess is as good as mine." I swallow down a mouthful of self-pity and look away.

"That must be so depressing," Amber says. "Sleeping with a bunch of dead heads."

"It isn't funny," I say. "Obviously my dreams are trying to tell me something."

"I'm not laughing," Amber says. "Why would I be? It seems like every time you have nightmares, someone close to you dies. Maybe I'm next."

"No one's next," I say. "I just need to figure out what everything means."

"I gotta go," Drea says. She grabs a bar of chocolate from her mini-fridge.

"Are you all right?" I ask.

"I don't know," she says. "I don't know if I can take another year of this." She swings her backpack over her shoulder and scoots out the door before I can say anything else.

"I gotta go, too," Amber says. She kicks through the mound of clothes at the foot of her bed. She picks up a peach sweatshirt, sniffs it, makes a "yuck" face, and then tosses it over her shoulder.

"What are you looking for?" I ask.

"Something to wear to yoga after school."

"Do you want to borrow something of mine?" I ask.

"Let's face it, Stace, your style's a bit too housewife for my chic blood."

"What's that supposed to mean?"

She grabs the box of Rice Krispies and pours a huge helping into her mouth before beginning the explanation.

And all the while she's talking, she's pointing at the big purple flower in her hair, flashing me the matching garter up around her thigh, and then gesturing toward my gray sweatshirt, draped over the chair—obviously trying to explain her laws of fashion. But I have absolutely no clue as to what she's saying because her mouth is completely Rice Krispied.

"Huh?" I feel my face twist up in confusion.

She garble-talks even louder, like that will make a difference. When she sees I still don't understand, she lets out a quacklike grunt, fishes a pair of pink stretch pants from the mound on the floor along with a couple tattered Hello Kitty notebooks, and heads out to class.

I, on the other hand, figure I can soak up another full block before heading off to Mrs. Halligan's happy couch. I hug my knees into my chest and glance down at my gingerbread-cookie-man pajamas, feeling a bit redeemed by their obvious cuteness. But then I look at the gaping hole in the knee from my fall up the stairs the other night. I poke my finger through it and take a deep breath.

I'd give anything to talk to Chad right now. I kind of wish I wasn't so hard on him about his surprise visit. I scooch back down in bed, feeling lonelier than I have in a long time. But I can't blame Drea and Amber for getting spooked and deserting me here. Who wants to room with the angel of death?

seven

When I arrive at Mrs. Halligan's office, she tells me to take a seat on the notorious happy sofa. Of course she doesn't actually call it that. She's dubbed it "the lounge"—an over-stuffed, green-and-yellow plaid number with wooden trim and worn-out arms. Anything but loungelike, but it's still the place she expects I'm going to spill it about everything that's going wrong in my life. Though I feel like that could take days.

"So," she begins, "your roommates tell me you had a bad dream this morning. Anything you want to talk about?"

She's sitting on a leather swivel chair, completely focused toward the tip of my nose from behind a pair of giant round eyeglasses. Big silver curls frame her face.

"Not really," I say.

She studies me a few seconds, legs crossed, old-lady shoe bobbing back and forth at me, hands folded neatly in her lap. "It's okay, Stacey," she says. "It's normal to experience nightmares after there's been some kind of trauma in your life. It's just your mind's way of dealing with the situation after the fact. We're coming up on a year now since last year's tragic events. That must be very hard for you."

This woman's a genius.

"Maybe this is just your body's way of exploring the experience," she continues. "Sometimes when something major or traumatic happens, our mind and body don't have time to ask questions."

"Ask questions?"

"Precisely," she nods, happy that I'm participating.

"Great!" I beam. "So I just need to let my mind and body ask the questions, find the answers, and then everything will go back to normal?" I tilt my head and nod to effect the degree of chipperness I'm going for.

"I know it might sound easier than it actually is, Stacey, but think about it. The next time you have a nightmare, ask yourself what you think your mind is trying to figure out. I think you'll be surprised with the result." She smiles at me and gives a slight nod of the head, confident in a job well done.

Once she gets me to promise to stop by later in the week—even though I know that won't happen—I'm free to go to D-block computers. Mr. Lecklider's got us all broken up into groups working on these huge, all-encompassing projects. While he sits at the back of the room playing round after round of Free Cell, my group—comprised of me and Amber and Cory and Emma (a couple of Hillcrest's newest recruits)—is working on a new Web site for the school.

"I wonder if we should scan in a picture of the cafeteria pizza," Amber says. "You know, so kids can see what kind of food we eat here."

To this, Emma blows her nose extra loud, as though enthused by the suggestion.

"Are you kidding?" Cory asks. "We actually want kids to come here."

"Then how about we scan in a picture of my ass?" Amber says.

"I repeat," he says. "We actually want kids to come here."

"I think the cafeteria pizza is good," Emma snorts between nose-blows.

"It *is* good." Amber hands Emma a fresh tissue from the box, replacing the tiny ball Emma has been recycling for the past ten minutes. "It's actually the only yummy food that comes out of the cafeteria."

"Forget it," Cory says. "We have enough pics."

Lucky for us, Cory is a major computer geek. He elected to take this class only for the easy A. So, while he packs the

Web site with everything from course descriptions to post-card-worthy pictures of the campus pond during sunset, I can browse the free e-cards on greetings4you.com. Since I was in major bitch mode the other morning with Chad, and since I won't get to see him until the last block of the day, I figure this is the quickest, most convenient way to say "I'm sorry."

I click through the array of sentiments—mice squeaking "I love you," cows mooing "I miss you," lovesick kissing fish, forget-me-not flowers, "you're my fuzzy-wuzzy" slippers, and numerous "I'm sweet on you" candies. I decide on one that's corny but cute: two pigs holding up a sign that says "hogs and kisses" while a peppy version of Louis Armstrong's "A Kiss to Build a Dream On" plays in the background.

I quickly turn the volume down on my computer, glance over my shoulder to make sure I haven't attracted Mr. Leck-lider's attention—I haven't—and begin typing my message:

> Dear Chad,
> Just a little note to tell you I'm sorry
> I freaked the other day. I'm glad you
> surprised me.
> Call me later.
> Hogs and kisses!
> Luv,
> Me

I click on the Send icon, feeling a smidgen better. I close the window and go into my e-mail account. There are five messages—two opportunities to work from home and make five thousand dollars per month, an offer to enlarge the body parts of my choice, this month's online issue of *TeenReads*, and a message from Silversorcerer198 marked "Stacey, we need to talk." I'm tempted to trash it, since I know no Silversorcerers whatsoever, but since I'm curious, I click it open.

"Dear Stacey," it reads. "Didn't mean to scare you the other morning in the boiler room. We need to talk. Meet me tonight at 11:30 at the Hangman Café."

A horrible, sticky feeling bubbles up in my throat.

"Stacey?" Amber says. "Why do you look as pale as my butt cheeks?"

I gesture to my computer screen. Amber rolls her chair beside me to look. "Holy Miss Molly," she says. "Do you think it's the same guy?"

"What else am I supposed to think?"

"What's up?" Cory asks. He leans in toward us, his shaggy, mud-brown hair hanging down the sides of his face.

"Girl stuff." Amber covers the screen with her hands, two big Porky Pig stickers stuck to her wrists.

"Show me," he says.

"I don't think so," Amber says.

"Well, then I don't think you guys will be receiving credit on this project," Cory says. "I *have* done all the work."

Emma inhales her concern.

"Fine," I say. "Look." I turn the monitor in his direction.

"You know the Hangman closes at eleven, don't you?" he says.

I feel the corners of my mouth sag down even further. I had forgotten the café's hours since we hardly ever hang out here.

"So, what does that mean?" Amber asks. "This guy wants to meet you after hours?"

"Maybe it's Donovan's successor." Cory stabs at the air with an invisible knife. "Maybe he wants to take revenge."

"And maybe you're, like, so immature," Amber says to him.

"You just don't want to admit the inevitable," Cory says. "I think this campus is cursed."

"Really?" Amber says.

"Think about it. The Hangman Café alone . . ."

"What about it?" Amber asks.

"You know that's not really the name, don't you? So, why do you think people call it that?"

"We know how the legend goes," Amber says. "We're not newbloods here, remember?"

"It's because some girl hung herself in there, right?" Emma blots at her nose with the tissue.

"Exactly," Cory says. His eyes are wide with excitement and his lips are practically frothing over from the sheer delight of this conversation. "Fifty years ago. When she didn't get the starring role in the school play. And then everything that happened last year with Veronica, splattered on the French room floor—"

"Shut up," I say, fighting the urge to block my ears.

"Tell me," he says. "Is it true that when you found Drea, she was tied up in a porta-potty?"

"Shut the hell up, geek boy," Amber hisses.

"I think there's more to come," he says. "And when it does, I just hope I'm around to see it."

Amber plucks the power cable from his computer, zapping away all the pretty pics.

"You little witch," he says. "Lucky for you I save my work every three minutes."

At that, Mr. Lecklider makes his way toward us, the heels of his shoes clicking against the linoleum floor. "Can I see what you're working on?"

"Amber just pulled the plug," Cory says.

"Well, that's a zero for all of you for today," Mr. Lecklider says. "And I'll see you all back here at 2:30 to continue your work."

"Oinkers," Amber says when Lecklider's out of earshot.

Cory plugs the cable back in and resumes our project in silence. Even though the guy is an ultimate jerk, his comments about the whole Hillcrest hysteria are hardly out of the ordinary. After Veronica's death, gobs of kids were pulled out of here by their parents. In return, we got a major transfusion of newbloods, kids like Cory—"ghost groupies" as Amber likes to call them—intrigued by all the negative press our school was getting, utterly delighted over the idea that the school might be haunted. And then some parents saw the major bailing of students as an opportunity for their beloved underachievers to get accepted.

It's almost as if everyone's just waiting for something to happen.

Everyone, including me.

eight

When I get to the cafeteria, Drea, Amber, and PJ are already sitting in our usual spot by the soda machines. I set my tray on the table and peel open the spout of my chocolate milk. "So, what's up?"

"Up?" Amber points toward the ceiling with her chopsticks.

"Yeah," I say. "What are you guys talking about?"

She plucks a chunk of potato from her salad and pokes it into her mouth. "You," she manages between chews.

"What about me?"

"The e-mail," Amber says. "Are you going tonight?"

I glance at Drea, who's focusing down at her plate of macaroni.

"I say go," PJ says, pointing with a cheese doodle for emphasis. "We'll all be there to back you up."

"Definitely," Amber says.

"Maybe we shouldn't talk about this now." I gesture to Drea, hoping they get the picture.

"What's with the silent treatment, Dray?" PJ asks. "You've been comatose-quiet since we got here."

"Nothing," she says.

"If it's nothing then why do you look as happy as a fried clam?" PJ asks.

"Maybe I'm just sick of listening to you guys act like this is some stupid Sega game," she says.

"It's not a game," Amber says. "It's a quest."

"A quest for a killer." PJ cackles. "And who his next victim will be."

"Who says it's a he?" Amber raises an eyebrow.

"So true, my little sly one." PJ clinks his fork against Amber's chopsticks, toastlike.

"What is wrong with you?" Drea pushes her tray away. "Was last year so long ago that you don't remember everything I went through?"

"We *all* went through it," Amber corrects.

"Okay, stop," I say, for Drea's sake. "That e-mail I got could just be some jerk trying to scare me after last year."

"He went through a lot of trouble," Amber says, "showing up in the boiler room and all. Writing 'M for Murder' on the window."

"I didn't say M was for murder." I look at Drea. She's got both hands pressed up against her forehead in headache mode.

"Um, yes you did," Amber corrects.

"Wasn't it you who thought all of that was a joke? A coincidence? The result of my being, quote unquote, 'funkified'?"

"I still think you're funkified," Amber says. "But you have to admit, after that e-mail you got, this has ghost groupie written all over it. I'll bet you anything it's one of them, just dying for some cheap thrill. No pun intended."

"I'll take some cheap thrill," PJ says, raising his hand.

"All I know," I say, "is that I'm dreaming about people who are already dead. If you ask me, that's a lot safer than dreaming about people who are going to die."

"I guess," Drea admits. She pulls her tray back and takes a bite of macaroni.

I wish Amber had the common sense not to go blabbing about my business. Drea isn't ready to hear about weird e-mail messages, not on top of boiler room break-ins, weird graffiti, and recurring nightmares. Which is why I haven't said anything about the puking. Because I'm thinking the puking isn't just merely coincidental. I think it's my body's way of trying to tell me something. Like last year—when wetting the bed turned out to be my body's way of leading me to where I'd find Drea, tied up in a porta-john.

I glance over at Donna Tillings, sitting alone at the end of our table. Her once auburn-highlighted hair is now pulled back in a rubber band, the color faded to a cheerless brown—like one of the "before" pictures in a magazine. It's weird; she never would have ventured a lipstick within a ten-foot radius of us last year, and now she's sitting at our table, with a face probably as blanched as mine.

Donna Tillings was Veronica Leeman's best friend—a class gossip to the core, the kind of girl only other bullies could stomach. After Veronica's death, she ended up shutting herself off from all her lemming friends. She took a couple weeks off to grieve, and instead of resuming old friendships when she returned, she tried to make new ones, tried to earn herself a fresh start. Only everyone who knew her knew they didn't like her. And for some reason, the influx of new students this year hasn't helped the situation any.

I blink my stare away and instead attempt to eat some of today's cafeteria fare—gluey clumps of mac and cheese with a dusting of readymade breadcrumbs on top. I'm just about to scoop a forkful into my mouth when a couple hands land across my eyes from behind.

It's Chad. I can smell him right away—the musky scent of his cologne mixed with the apple-butter soap I bought him as a just-because gift last month.

"What are you doing here?" I can hear the excitement in my voice.

Chad moves his hands away and scoots into the seat beside me. "I got your e-mail."

"You did?"

He nods. "Thank you."

"I shouldn't have freaked," I say.

"No," he argues, "I should have told you I was coming instead of just showing up like that."

"Aren't they the cutest?" Amber coos, referring to me and Chad. She tilts her head, all dreamylike.

The interruption of her voice reminds me of where I am and who's here. I can feel Drea's eyes watching us, watching Chad tickling my side.

"Hey Drea," he says, sensing my discomfort, I think.

"Hi," she mumbles, really sticking it to that macaroni.

"I should probably get back to Spanish." He flashes me the obscene wooden bathroom pass in his pocket—a giant phallus-shaped key that Señora Sullivan insists is supposed to look like a bean burrito—and then peers over his shoulder to make sure Mrs. Amsler, the cafeteria warden, hasn't noticed him. "I'll call you tonight after the hockey game." He gives me a tiny peck on the cheek before sneaking out the side exit door.

I glance back up at Drea, who's focusing on her plate as though the pasta noodles hold all the answers. I have no idea what she's more upset about—me and Chad or this whole nightmare business. I just know we need to have a serious talk.

nine

After school, Amber and I end up going straight to yoga class. I figure an hour of mind-centering postures might help melt a bit of the tension I feel building up inside of me. And, for the most part, I think it works. As Keegan, our RD/yoga instructor, leads us through a series of warm-ups and then *vinyasas*, I feel the tension begin to dissipate.

I cover myself with a wool blanket and lie flat on my back in preparation for *Savasana*. It's sort of ironic that this is actually my favorite part of yoga—ironic because Savasana is also sometimes referred to as the corpse pose. I close my eyes and try to forget I know this bit of trivia. I'm beyond tired so it's actually not so difficult to just let my mind go numb. I concentrate on the musical chanting in the background, mixed with the hum of the aquarium filter, and slowly begin to feel myself drift into lovely space.

But then I remember. I sit up straight and look down at my watch. I forgot about Lecklider's detention. I peel myself off the sticky mat, grab my bag, and plow through the doors without even bothering to tell Amber to come along with me. Halfway down the hallway, I manage to get my sneakers on, still doing my best to move toward the classroom. But when I get there, there's an e-mail note tacked up on the door announcing that detention has been moved to the basement.

I hurry my way down two flights of steps and charge through the steel door at the bottom. There's a wooden sign that reads DETENTION FOR STACEY BROWN hanging on the wall. It points down the long and narrow hallway that faces me.

I begin making my way in that direction, wondering why the sign only lists my name—why I'm the only one with detention down here.

The sparse, yellow overhead lights cast down over a hallway littered with custodial debris—paint cans, rollers, rags, some mixing sticks, a custodial uniform balled up on the floor. The walls and floor are a deep green color, just a layer of paint over bare cement, and there are doors on the right and left. I try the closest door to the left. Locked. I try another. Also locked. I continue down the hallway, listening at a few of the doors, trying the knobs. But it's like this place is completely deserted.

Like maybe this has been a mistake.

I'm just about to turn around and head back when I hear something coming from the end of the hallway. It's a slapping sound, like someone's feet hitting against the cement floor.

"Hello?" I call.

The slapping stops.

The end of the hallway is still several yards away. I take a few steps closer, noticing a large gray door at the very end. "Hello?" I call again.

Still nothing.

I wonder if maybe this whole thing is yet another stupid joke, if maybe someone's watching me right now, trying to hold in a fit of laughter. I look around, toward the ceiling and then behind me.

"Hello?" I call out again. "This isn't funny."

No response.

I turn to leave, walking quickly at first, but then gathering speed.

The slapping sound starts up again; I can hear it echoing off the walls. I hurtle through the steel basement door at full speed and scramble up the stairs in complete darkness, the lights in the stairwell all switched off. There's a set of doors at the top. I feel for the handles and try pushing them, but it's like they're chained. Like I'm trapped.

I pound my fists against the doors, kick at the handles to try and break the lock, yell with all the energy I have for someone to come and help me. But it's deathly quiet.

The steel door to the basement opens. The sound of footsteps makes its way toward me, up the stairs. I squat down in the corner.

"Stacey?" says a male voice. "Are you here?"

I don't say anything.

"It's okay," he says. "It's just me."

I squint to try and make out a face, like that will make a difference.

"It's me," he insists. "I knew I'd find you here."

"PJ?" I call out.

I wait several seconds before beginning my way back down the stairs. "Where are you?" I walk through the door at the bottom. Still no one. "PJ?" I call out. I can hear someone laughing at the end of the hallway. Why is he doing this? How is this supposed to be funny?

I start down the hallway again, following the sound of laughter. It leads me closer to the slapping sound. Maybe I should just go to it. Maybe the answer to getting out of here is behind it.

Focusing on the weathered gray door at the end, I wonder if it might be the way out. It seems darker the closer I get to it, the yellowy overhead lights more dim and sparse. I keep moving toward the door, the sound of the slapping getting louder, so close now. I take several steps, squinting to make out the shadows that play to the right of the door. They jump back and forth to the beat of the slapping. Like someone's there. Waiting for me.

"Hello?" I call.

Just a few yards away now, I can make out a looplike shadow against the door. And just to the right of it, scribbled on the ground in a dark red color, is a giant letter M. It's staring right up at me.

"Stacey," says a girl's voice.

I freeze. There's a walloping inside my chest, pushing through my skin, freezing me in place. I know that voice. I'd recognize it anywhere. But it can't be. Maura's dead. She's been dead for four years.

"Stacey," Maura's voice repeats.

Tears roll down the sides of my face. My stomach bubbles up in fear and pain. I want to be sick. I hold my gut and try to calm the quake in my stomach.

"Whatsa matter?" she asks. "Tummy ache?"

The shadow of the loop continues in a perpetual motion, from top to bottom, and then rotates around, like a jump rope. I move up to the door. But no one's there, just the jumping shadow. And I can hear her voice, singing that "Miss Mary Mack" song I taught her—except the words are much different:

> Miss Mary Mack, Mack, Mack, all dressed in black, black, black. She has a knife, knife, knife, stuck in her back, back, back. She cannot breathe, breathe, breathe. She cannot cry, cry, cry. That's why she begs, begs, begs. She begs to die, die, die.

"Who's there?" I cry out. "Who's doing this? Why is this happening?"

The singing stops, but then I hear Maura scream. I pound and kick against the door, but I'm going to be sick. I can't hold it in.

"Stacey," a male voice whispers through the door crack. "Will you keep your promise?"

"What?" I shriek. "What are you talking about?"

"In less than one week," the voice says.

My mouth arches to scream but instead fills with bile. Vomit. Spurting out my mouth.

"Stacey!" I feel a tug at my arm.

"She's in there!" I blurt out when my throat clears. "Jumping rope."

"Stacey!" Amber repeats, shaking me out of dreamland, to my senses.

I look around, finally coming to, my heart thrashing in my chest. We're still in yoga class.

Keegan hovers over me, the silver ends of her long, dark corkscrew hair hitting against my arm, giving me the chills. "Are you okay?"

"Yeah." I wipe the vomit from the corners of my mouth and see a puddle of it on the sticky mat beside me. "I guess something just didn't agree with me."

She nods. "Why don't you go to the bathroom and clean yourself up?"

"It's like I always say," Amber begins, "cafeteria food mixed with body contortions is *so* not a good idea."

I get up and make my way to the bathroom, noticing I've interrupted even the most dedicated yoga practitioners from their corpselike Savasana. I close the door behind me and splash some water on my face, doing my best to ease my senses, to wash out my mouth with my finger. I look in the mirror and stare deeply into my golden-brown eyes—

eyes just like my grandmother's. Hers held strength and courage, and weren't afraid to see. But mine are simply covered over with redness, angry veins stretching across the pupils. I look down at the amethyst ring she gave me—a square and chunky stone that almost reaches my knuckle. And then it hits me.

I have less than a week to figure out why I'm dreaming about old ghosts. Because if I don't, someone could end up dead.

ten

Amber and I are back in our room, sitting crosslegged on my bed, and I've just guzzled down practically a whole two-liter bottle of ginger ale.

Amber refolds the dampened rag and hands it to me. "So—we need to talk. Drea's not here. What's going on for real?"

"What do you mean?"

"Look, Stacey," she says, rolling her eyes. "I'm not stupid. I know you fell asleep in yoga class. And I know that sleep plus weird bodily functions equals some serious bad kitty for you."

"Huh?" I rub at the throb in my head.

"Don't go getting all denial on me about it. Between this afternoon and this morning's freak show in the common room . . . What's going on? And what, can I ask, was up with that twisted little song you were singing?"

"What are you talking about?"

"In yoga class . . . I assume when you fell asleep. You were singing some dirgeful version of 'Miss Mary Mack.'"

"I was?"

She nods. "Like straight out of the Addams Family show tunes."

This time I tell her everything—all the details about the nightmare I had in yoga class and how, yes, it's true, my nightmares have been making me sick to my stomach.

Contrary to her earlier behavior in the cafeteria with PJ, Amber looks about as disappointed as I feel. She grabs her feather-fringed pillow off the floor and begins plucking away at the individual quills.

"What happened to 'a quest for a killer'?" I ask. "You seemed so into it earlier."

"That was BP," she says.

"BP?"

"Yeah, you know," she holds up a feather for emphasis. "Before the Puke. The purposeful puking changes everything. Now I know it's bad kitty. It's just like last year, with your icky bedwetting."

"Yeah, well, if it hadn't been for that bedwetting, I may have never saved Drea; I may never have been able to find her."

"So how's the puking supposed to help us?" She sighs. "And who's in trouble this time?"

"I don't know. But like I said before, I think it's better to be dreaming about people who are already dead than people who are going to die, don't you?"

"All I know is that it so sucks for you," she says. "I mean, I can't even handle the Monthly Marvin, never mind bedwetting one year and impromptu puking the next. How do you do it, Stacey? How do you even manage to get out of bed each day?"

I blot my eyes with the rag, finally noticing that it's actually a dampened thong with a scowling, buxom Wonder Woman silkscreened on the front. "What is this?"

"It was the only clean thing I could find."

At that, the door to our room opens. It's Drea. I quickly stuff the thong-rag under my covers.

"What's up?" She deposits her backpack on the floor and sits down on the edge of her bed, facing us.

"Not much," I say.

"Really?" Drea purses her lips together. "Why don't I believe you?"

"I don't know." Amber pokes a feather behind her ear. "Maybe it's because you're paranoid."

"Maybe," Drea says. "Or maybe it's because Stacey upchucked in yoga class. You don't think people aren't talking about it?"

"Great." I flop back against my pillow, grab the thong-rag from under the covers, and lay it over my eyes in a futile attempt to block everything out.

While the two discuss the highlights of my vomit, I do my best to concentrate on why my nightmares are making me sick. And then it occurs to me. I didn't get sick when I dreamt about Veronica. So what makes that nightmare different? I try to think, but I just can't concentrate.

"Wait," Amber shouts. "Stacey, maybe you threw up because of morning sickness."

"Oh, please," I moan.

"What?" I can hear the smile in Amber's voice. "It makes total sense, doesn't it? And it's completely possible, isn't it? *Isn't it?*"

"I don't feel like talking about this." I can just picture Drea's face in my mind—jaw locked, teeth clenched, eyes rolled up toward the ceiling.

"Come on," Amber pleads.

"Forget it," I say.

"Well, that answers my question," she sighs. "If you can't talk about it, obviously you haven't done it."

"Not that it's any of your business," I begin, "but me and Chad are perfectly happy with our PG-13 relationship."

"Tell *him* that," Amber says.

I remove the thong-rag from my eyes and scoot up in bed. Drea has already changed from her uniform into civilian clothes—a pair of low-rise jeans paired with the most basic of basic-blue turtleneck tops, her hair knotted up in one of those big plastic clips. So why does she look so damned perfect?

"Coming to dinner?" she asks, fishing her school ID from the side pocket of her backpack.

But since I definitely need some alone time, I tell them about my grandiose plans to make a microwave version of a grilled-cheese sandwich here—even though there's a giant part of me that doesn't want a dolled-up Drea to have such open access to my boyfriend.

After they leave, I roll over in bed and stare at the bright white candle on the night table, wondering if this might be an opportune time to light it—since I feel so alone, since I'd give almost anything to talk to my grandmother right now. But instead I grab the phone and dial my mother.

She answers. "Hello?"

"Hi, Mom." I tug the covers up over my cheek and do my best to hold back the tears I feel storming up inside me. We talk for several minutes about normal stuff—about school and my teachers, about the season premiere of *Gilmore Girls* and the new painting class she's taking. I almost want to tell her about my Maura nightmares. But I don't. Because I know she won't understand. Because we get along best when I don't talk about my visions—when I'm least like my grandmother, when I try my best to separate myself from witchdom.

After a good twenty-plus minutes of pauseless conversation, we end up saying our goodbyes and hanging up—she, completely pleased with our healthy relationship, and me, completely repressed by it.

eleven

In lieu of dinner, I've decided to brew up some prophecy tea. I pull the family scrapbook from the back of my closet in hopes of finding a good recipe. The book was given to me by my grandmother just two weeks before she passed away. It's crammed with all sorts of spells and home remedies, verses of favorite poetry, and secret recipes from those in my family before me.

I don't use the book very often, frankly, because I feel very strongly that spells come from within, that the most effective spells are those we create ourselves. But sometimes I do like to use it. I like the book's sense of connection. I like to run my fingers over the handwritten pages and dream about the people who wrote them—what their lives might have been like, what might have prompted them to write a given spell or scribble down a certain recipe in the first place.

I set the weighty book down on my bed and flip through its yellowing pages. On a half-burned piece of tracing paper, I find a recipe for prophecy tea written by great-great-aunt Delia.

I place a bowl of water atop the dresser and add the necessary ingredients: a pinch of cinnamon, two teaspoons of nutmeg for luck, three squeezes of a lime, and a few dried saffron petals.

I grab a wooden spoon from my spell drawer, mix everything up, and then set the bowl in the microwave for a full five minutes. The water is steaming when I take it out. I sit back on my bed with the bowl positioned in my lap, and allow the curls of steam to lap over my face. The cinnamon scent, like sweet wood, washes over my senses and opens them up. I close my eyes and concentrate on the saffron petals blending with the lime. The juice from the lime will help cleanse away any negative energy that might be looming over me from last year, while the saffron will help increase my psychic awareness.

I open my eyes and mix everything up once more with the spoon, concentrating on the blending of ingredients and what their unification means. I lift the bowl to my lips and take a sip. It tastes like holidays, like licking the batter bowl clean after my mother has made Gram's recipe for cinnamon twirl puffs. The whole process soothes me, grounds me, makes me feel empowered, like maybe I can do this again.

With just a few sips left, I hear the door squeak open. It's Drea.

"Hi," she says, not really looking at me.

"Hi." I feel my back straighten.

"I just came back for a book," she says. "I'm meeting a study group in the library."

"Can we talk?"

"I really don't have time. They're already waiting for me." She grabs a couple textbooks from her desk and stuffs them into her backpack, still avoiding eye contact.

"Please."

She pauses from packing and purses her lips, focusing on the area above my head. "Amber told me about the puking, Stacey. How it happened *after* you fell asleep, and how you guys are convinced something else is gonna happen. I just can't handle it right now."

"I understand," I say, practically biting through my tongue. "But that's not what I wanted to talk about."

"Oh," she says. "Then what?"

I scoot toward the edge of my bed. "I just feel like there's been some weird energy between us lately."

"I'm not one of your failed spells, Stacey."

"I never said you were." I gulp down what's left of my tea. "It's just that today in the cafeteria when Chad came by, even the other morning when he came to visit, I felt that you were sort of . . ."

"What?"

"I don't know. I guess sort of upset or something."

"I'm not jealous about Chad, if that's what you're thinking."

"Okay," I say. "I mean, I'm glad. Because I think if it were me, I might be jealous." I catch myself squeezing and resqueezing the lime wedges into my empty mug for no apparent reason. "I was trying to imagine how it would be, you know, to have a best friend date your ex."

"It doesn't bother me," she says, twisting a strand of blond hair around her finger. "Me and Chad were over ages ago."

"Are you sure?"

Drea lowers her eyes to look at me finally, and, for just a second, I think she might cry, but instead she nods—a slight, less-than-believable up-and-down shake to the head. Our eyes stay locked on one another until we're interrupted by Amber.

She slams the door shut behind her. "You'll never believe what just happened to me." She's liplinered two pink ghosts to her cheeks with big Xs over them.

"What?" Drea lets out a relieved sigh, perhaps grateful for the interruption.

"Well," Amber begins, "I was on my way back from the mailboxes and this guy who I've never even seen before, probably some transfer dork—one of the ghost groupies— crashes right into me, making me drop all my mail. So, then, as he's helping me pick it back up, he tells me to have a happy anniversary and asks me how I'll be celebrating."

I lock eyes with Drea, catching sight of her trembling lip. She bites it and looks away again.

"So, what did you say?" I ask.

"I asked him what he was talking about," Amber says. "I mean, I know it's the anniversary, I just wasn't thinking . . . and then he tells me that he and his friend are going to try and break into O'Brian and perform some séance or something."

O'Brian is the academic building where Veronica was killed. It happened in Madame Lenore's French room, on the first floor. The administration ended up boarding up the room and closing off that part of the building right after it happened. But kids, convinced the place was haunted, refused to take classes anywhere near the building. And so for a while it just sort of sat there, like a constant reminder of what happened. But now, with much monetary support from rich parents and other donors, it's being renovated—new paint, new floors, a new computer facility—like a million-dollar makeover will wipe away the horrific events of the past and make the parents happy.

"I hate this school," Drea says. "I should have transferred when I had the chance."

I stand up and go to drape my arm around Drea's shoulder, but she tugs away slightly.

"Here's your mail." Amber extracts a thick wad from her stack and hands it to me.

"Why do you have *my* mail?"

"*Why?*" Amber snaps her blueberry gum. "Because I picked it up. Why else?"

Even though I trust Amber, I hate the idea of anyone going through my stuff. I snatch the stack from her clutches, purposely neglecting to thank her for the gesture.

"You're welcome," she says anyway, as though reading my mind.

I thumb through the individual pieces—a telephone bill, a spell-supply catalog, this month's issue of *Teen People*, and a letter. The letter is in a business-sized envelope, with no return address. It just has my name and the school address typed in the middle.

My fingers tremble. I turn the letter over and press along the creases of the glued flap. The negative vibrations move down my palms and ice over my skin, like static of some sort. I try to swallow, but my mouth feels like it's full of paste, like I can't breathe, like I'm going to be sick. The letter drops from my fingertips.

"Stacey—" Amber reaches out to me. "What is it?"

I shake my head.

Amber motions to pick the letter up.

"No!" I shout.

"Why?" she asks. "What is it?"

But I can't say it, don't want to admit it, what I'm sensing.

I grab the bowl of dried lavender from beside my bed and press my fingertips against the pellets. I breathe the soothing scent in, doing my best to remind myself of inner strength.

Amber comes and sits beside me on the bed, which prompts Drea to join me as well.

"It's gonna be okay," Drea says, pushing the hair back from my face.

But I'm not so sure.

Still, with the lavender and their friendship combined, I'm able to take a deep breath, to swallow normally, and pick the letter up. I hold it in both hands, focusing down on my name, so black against the paper's creamy whiteness.

I slip my finger under the corner flap and tear across the top.

"Are you sure?" Amber asks.

I nod, carefully dipping my fingers into the envelope to pull the letter out. Drea grips around my shoulders extra tight as I unfold it.

WILL YOU KEEP YOUR PROMISE?

Amber reads the typed words aloud. "What does it mean? What promise?"

I shake my head because I don't know either. Because the same words were spoken aloud in my nightmare. And I have no idea what to do about it.

twelve

I sit on the edge of the bed shaking, like a cold chill has come and blanketed itself over my neck and back. Amber nestles the comforter over my shoulders, and Drea sets a second mug of water into the microwave for some tea. I just want to put this all away—to go to sleep and have blank, unimpressionable dreams. But I know that just won't happen.

I clutch the letter in my hands and stare down at the words, typed in caps, dead center of the page. I can almost hear the voice in my nightmare saying these words to me.

"The letter was postmarked here." Amber holds the envelope out for me to see, the red postmark ink with the town's name, Hanover, pressed over the stamp.

"Maybe it's just somebody from school," Drea says. "You know, another prank."

"Pranks don't give off vibes like that," I say.

Drea hands me the mug of tea and I sip it down in even gulps, savoring the sweet, orangey flavor.

"So you have no idea what the letter's referring to?" Amber asks. "What the promise is?"

"No," I say. "But the same question was in my nightmare."

"What do you mean?" Drea asks.

"I mean, in my nightmare, I heard someone's voice; it asked me if I'd keep my promise. It also said 'in less than one week.'"

"In less than what week, *what*?" Drea asks.

"I don't know."

"What did the voice sound like?" Amber asks. "Did you recognize it?"

"It was a male voice, I think. But I don't remember anything distinct about it. It could have been anyone."

"So we obviously need to figure out what this promise is," Amber says.

"I know."

"Do you have any idea at all?"

I lean back against the headboard to think. I wonder if it's something I promised to Maura, to her family, that I'm not remembering. Why else would I be dreaming about her? Or maybe it's something more recent. Did I promise something last year, after Veronica's death, that I just let fade from my mind?

"I just don't know," I sigh.

"Maybe you promised someone you'd help them," Drea says.

I stare up at a blank ceiling. "This is so completely frustrating."

"Maybe you need food," Amber says. "That usually helps *me* think." She grabs the box of Rice Krispies from her desk and holds it out to me as an edible Band-Aid.

"No thanks."

"We'll figure this out," she says, plopping down beside me and pouring a handful of Krispies into her palm.

"There's only one way." I sit back up.

"What are you talking about?" Drea nibbles at her acrylic fingernails.

"I have to go tonight."

"Where?" Drea asks.

"The Hangman," I say, feeling my chest tighten. "To meet whoever sent that e-mail. To see what he—or she—wants."

"Are you sure?" Amber asks.

I nod. "He obviously has something to tell me."

"Well, you're not going alone." Amber rests a hand on my shoulder.

"Thanks," I say, managing a smile.

"You'll come too, right, Dray?" Amber asks.

But Drea is looking away. "I don't know if I can," she says, in a voice as tiny as the snap, crackle, and popping going on in Amber's mouth right now.

"No," I say, turning to Drea. "I don't expect you to go. As a matter of fact, I think it's best if you stay here. Just in case something happens . . . we know we can reach you."

"And you'll know where we've gone," Amber adds. "Just in case we don't come back."

"Stop it," I say. "We'll be fine."

"Are you sure?" Drea asks.

"Definitely."

Drea smiles and I smile back, like maybe the tension of the situation has helped alleviate some of the weird energy between us.

"What time did the e-mail say again?" Amber asks.

"Eleven-thirty."

"You still have a couple hours," Drea says.

"So what should we do?" Amber asks.

"Do you want to call Chad to go with you guys?" Drea asks. "Or maybe we should call campus police to give them the heads up."

"I think I just need some time to myself." The letter still in my hand, I grab an afghan from my bed and a handful of dried orange peels from the jar in my spell drawer. I make my way out to the sofa in the common room. I need complete silence to concentrate, to pour my energy into the letter and hope that it comes back to me per the law of three—Gram used to always remind me that whatever energy I cast out into the universe would come back at me three times.

I lay the letter open on the coffee table in front of me and drop the orange peels on it. I arrange the peels in the shape of the sun—one circular piece in the center with twisted, narrow spokes that radiate from it for rays. I concentrate on the idea of the sun, on the sun's energy and its ability to awaken the senses. My grandmother used to say that I would always do my best studying outside because the sun's energy would enliven me. And that, in times when the sun is down, I should bring it back up with something symbolic that reminds me of its power and energy.

I rub each individual peel between the tips of my fingers, thinking how the sun implanted its energy into the peel to bring about the orangey color, to give birth to the fruit inside. Then I close my eyes, collect the peels into my lap, and run my fingers over the letter, transferring the sun's energy from my skin to the grain of the paper. I feel the individual creases, the way the letter was folded up in three. For some reason it urges me to fold it up even more. I go with the feeling, folding the letter up into a palm-sized square, tucking and untucking flaps until I end up with that MASH game I used to play in grade school.

"Let me guess." A much-uninvited Trish Cabone comes and plops herself down on the sofa beside me. "Stacey Brown will marry Chad McCaffrey, they'll have three children, live in a mansion, and have chimpanzees for pets."

I feign a polite giggle. "You're obviously familiar with MASH."

"Totally." She pulls at the clump of curlicues atop her head—tight black ringlets with just a hint of midnight blue—and props her elephant-slippered feet up on the table. "MASH fortunes were the most fun. Of course, that was when I was twelve."

"Right," I say, pocketing the letter and my orange peels. I have no idea what prompted me to fold the letter up that way. "I guess I was just seeing if I remembered how to play."

"You and Chad are pretty serious, aren't you? So maybe you guys will get married."

I shrug.

She yanks at the wad of watermelon-pink gum in her mouth and nods her head emphatically, like my silent shrugging is so profound.

"I better go study. History test tomorrow."

"Wait," she says, her eyes all big and round, thick black rings of liner outlining the lids. "I wanted to ask you, what was up with the other night? You know . . . when you started screaming out here?"

"Just a bad nightmare," I say, getting up.

"About last year?" She stands up as well. "A lot of kids have been talking about it, you know?"

I nod.

"Was your nightmare like one of the ones you were having last year? About Drea?"

"No," I manage. "It was different than that."

"Different how?" She's pulling at her curls again. "Like, different because it *felt* different? Or different because you weren't dreaming about Drea this time? Maybe you were dreaming about someone else?"

"I think I have a headache." I turn on my heel, making an attempt to beeline it back to my room, but Trish's prying questions force me to stop.

"I heard about yoga class," she says. "Were you dreaming then? About someone jumping rope? About somebody being trapped maybe? Didn't you scream those things out? Weren't you chanting some weird verse?" She starts humming the "Miss Mary Mack" tune.

I turn around to face her and she stops humming.

"They're doing some special service in the chapel Thursday night, you know?" she says. "Some people were wondering if you're gonna go. Are you?"

Why didn't I hear about any service? Have I been so out of it these past few days that I've failed to pay attention to what's going on outside my head?

"We could go together if you want," she continues. "I mean, I didn't know Veronica, being new here and all, but I just thought it would be the right thing to do. Is Drea going?"

Is she serious? Does she really expect me to go with her—an obvious ghost groupie?

"I don't think that's a good idea," I say.

"Maybe not," she says. "Maybe your presence might upset some people, you know? It must be hard for you, showing your face around here after letting Veronica just die like that."

"I didn't *let* her die."

"You didn't try so hard to save her either."

A direct hit. Before she can crawl any deeper under my skin, I turn around, walk into my room, and close the door.

thirteen

Before we head over to the Hangman, I've asked Amber to
help me remember the words to the "Miss Mary Mack"
song I was singing in yoga class. We're sitting on my bed
with a notebook between us, a giant letter *M* written in red
at the top of the page, and the words to the song in the
middle.

Drea is doing her best to block us out. She's got her foot
propped up on a pre-calc book while she reads *CosmoGirl*,

French-manicures her toenails, and hums along to the tunes pumping through her Discman.

"Totally creepy," Amber says, reading over the lines of the song. "I can just imagine what people are thinking."

"I already know what they're thinking," I say. "That I'm Linda Blair possessed by the devil."

"Linda Blair?"

"Yeah, you know, *The Exorcist* . . . the girl who pukes up green gunk and then her head spins around?"

"So right." Amber giggles. She grabs her square black glasses and sets the notebook down in her lap. "*Miss Mary Mack, Mack, Mack,*" she sings. "*All dressed in black, black, black. She has a knife, knife, knife, stuck in her back, back, back. She cannot breathe, breathe, breathe. She cannot cry, cry, cry. That's why she begs, begs, begs. She begs to die, die, die.*"

"I wonder what it means."

"'A knife stuck in her back'?" Amber questions. "I wonder if it means betrayal of some sort, you know? Like, watch your back."

I shrug. "Why can't she breathe or cry?"

"Maybe she's being gagged or suffocated in some way."

"And that's why she begs to die." I swallow hard and focus down on the letter *M*, wondering if it does indeed stand for murder.

"I don't know," Amber says. "Maybe we're taking the song too literally, you know? Like, one time I had this dream that I was being chased by tiny baby corn."

"And?"

"And I obviously didn't think that that was going to happen. I mean, I don't even *like* baby corn."

"Maybe that's why it was chasing you," I joke.

"Exactly," she says, lowering the glasses to the tip of her nose, staring at me over the frames. "I think it was my brain's way of saying I should try baby corn, you know? Be more adventurous with my veggie intake."

"Does this phallic little dream of yours have a point?"

"The point *is* that sometimes a baby corn is just a baby corn."

"Translation, please."

Amber rolls her eyes. "Why read so far into it? I mean, maybe this is just your brain's way of telling you that you're scared. Just about every scary movie has at least *someone* getting a knife shoved in their back—most often a clumsy bottle blond with lots of cleavage—but *still*, it's scary."

"I *do* know that I'm scared." I wipe the corner of my eye and look away.

"I know." She pulls a tissue from the front of her shirt and holds it out as an offering.

"No, thanks." I take a deep breath and rip the page out of the notebook. I fold it up into a tight little ball—as small as I can get it.

"What are you doing?" Amber asks.

"Making the fear more manageable." I grab a piece of cheesecloth, a bottle of dried thyme, and a stick of sandal-wood incense from my spell drawer. I drop the paper ball into the center of the cloth and then sprinkle the thyme on it—until I feel my fear retreat, until I feel confident I can overpower it. The green and brown bits of thyme, like the tiniest dried-out twigs, form a heap over the paper ball. I wrap it all up in the cloth and secure it with a rubber band.

"It's a courage sachet," I say, holding it up for Amber. "For tonight."

"Maybe pepper spray would work better," Amber says, stuffing the tissue back into her bra.

"Very funny." I light the incense and then charge the sachet by passing it three times through the smoke, the sweet woodsy smell helping to ease my nerves even more.

"Okay," I say, finally. "I'm ready."

.　　.　　.

Against Drea's better judgment, Amber and I make our way over to the Hangman by ourselves. It just seems easier this way, rather than getting other people involved. Plus, if whoever sent that e-mail message sees me trudging over with an entourage in tow, campus police included, I can be fairly certain he'll make himself scarce. Who wouldn't?

And so, the courage sachet in hand, Amber and I schlep our way across campus, walking between buildings to avoid open areas, doing our best to avoid campus police cruisers navigating the area. We even end up taking a detour by the library, making it the longest route possible—anything to avoid having to pass by the O'Brian building at night.

"I can't believe how cold it is tonight," Amber says, breaking the tension. She stuffs her hands into her pockets.

"We're almost there," I tell her.

The Onstage Café, better known amongst students as "the Hangman," is just ahead of us. A cream-colored houselike building with a pointed roof, it once served as the school theater. But after that girl hung herself, it's become the campus coffee shop/study lounge—sort of a bleak thought.

"Do you think they're still serving hot cocoa?" Amber asks.

"Not if they're closed," I say.

"Maybe whoever sent the e-mail works there and can get us in. Maybe he already has some cocoa made up for us."

I ignore Amber's wishful thinking and continue toward the main glass doors. I can see there are lights on in the back, by the cash register, but it's completely dark in the seating areas, both the elevated stage section and the lower audience part.

"Should we knock?" Amber whispers.

"He might not even be inside." I look over my shoulder toward the path where we walked.

"That would be, like, so completely cruel," Amber says. "Tempting us here with the thought of hot cocoa and biscotti, only to make us rot out in the cold."

"Are you for real?" I whisper back. "Did you forget why we're here?"

Amber rolls her eyes. "It's called trying to make the best of the situation." She moves closer to the door and knocks.

"No!" I mouth.

"Why? I don't have all night to wait for this dork." She continues to pound at the door, the faux-fur body of her leopard-print coat bundled tightly around her.

"No!" I repeat. "You'll draw attention to us."

"Look, Stacey," Amber presses the light of her ladybug watch to illuminate the time and holds it out for me to see.

"It's *after* 11:30. Either this geek comes out and gets serious, or I'm outta here. I think my tongue is icing over."

I'll have to admit, she's right about the weather. I think it's the coldest November we've ever had. But that doesn't mean I'm willing to get caught out here after curfew.

"Okay," I say, squeezing my sachet of courage. "Let's make a deal. How about you stop knocking and wait here to see if anyone comes. I'll go check out the area around the building. If we don't see anything, we'll leave." I pull a flashlight from my backpack.

"Fine," Amber agrees.

I move over to the side of the building and aim the flashlight over shrubbery, among trees scattered about the lawn, and toward the brick walkway that loops back to the main buildings. But it just looks vacant. So maybe Drea was right. Maybe this is just one huge prank. Maybe the anniversary of what happened last year is really bringing out the worst in people—maybe even bringing out the worst in my nightmares.

I turn to move back toward the front of the building. That's when I notice two thick bands of light moving forward along the ground, like the beams of large flashlights. I peek around the side of the building and see Amber, obviously trying to explain herself to two campus police officers.

"I think I left my sweater in there," I hear her say. "It's my favorite. A Stella McCartney original. I can't just let it sit in there. Someone will thief it for sure."

"Are you out here alone?"

"Yup." She looks over her shoulder in my direction. "All alone."

Unfortunately, her bogus attempt at lying tips them off. One of the officers shines his light in my direction just moments before I'm able to duck my head.

Great.

Instead of succumbing to the humiliation of having him drag me out to the front of the building, I go willingly.

"Sorry," I say to the bigger of the two. "My friend forgot her sweater inside, and I just came along so she wouldn't have to be out alone."

"Then what were you doing at the side of the building?" he asks.

A good question. "I was trying to peek into the side windows to see if I could see it."

The younger officer, the one who looks like he just walked off the pages of an Abercrombie & Fitch catalog— tanned face, broad chest, dark wavy hair that dangles over a set of the most deliciously chocolate-brown eyes—shines his mother-of-a-flashlight into the building, illuminating a face.

Cory's face.

"Computer dork!" Amber exclaims.

He's wearing an apron, like he actually works here. He pulls a key ring from his pocket to unlock the door. "What's going on?" he asks, focusing a moment on the ghosts still liplinered on Amber's face. "I was just cleaning up out back."

"Where's Mr. Gunther?" Mr. Abercrombie & Fitch asks. "Isn't he in charge of closing up the café?"

Mr. Gunther is Hillcrest's suspender-wearing, knuckle-cracking, way-too-much-cologne-wearing algebra teacher.

"He wasn't feeling well tonight and had to leave early." Cory grimaces, like he just got Gunther in trouble.

Officer Abercrombie jots the detail down in his notepad before focusing back on Cory. "Is anyone coming to close up for him?"

"No," Cory says. "I mean, it's no big deal. All I have to do is shut off the lights and lock the door. Gunther knows I'm responsible."

The officer nods, I think, mulling over whether or not to buy the story.

"Brrr . . ." Amber folds her arms in front. "I could sure use an extra coat." She eyes Officer Abercrombie's jacket. "Or maybe we should all go inside and discuss this over hot cocoa. I know *I've* got time." She pouts her lips, super-model-style, arches her eyebrows approvingly at his puffed-out chest, and then looks him in the eye. But that *still* fails to nab his attention, which prompts her next desperate attempt. She starts doing this ridiculous little dance to show just *how* cold she really is—feet tapping, head bobbing from side to side, arms flapping like chicken wings.

"Did you happen to find a sweater in there while you were cleaning?" the officer, obviously completely immune to Amber's idea of seduction, asks Cory.

Cory shakes his head and makes a face—cheeks sagging and mouth all droopy—as though he's completely baffled by this whole scene.

"Fine," the officer says. "Are you almost done?"

Cory nods. "Yeah, I'm just finishing up."

"Well, I'll wait while you finish and then give you a ride back to your dorm."

Amber's face drops. And I know exactly why. It isn't because it could possibly be Cory who sent me that e-mail. Nor is it because it was he who forced me to let him read the e-mail in the first place, who knew all along we would show up here at this exact time. It's because Mr. Hunky-Abercrombie-&-Fitch police officer is going to hang around and wait to give Cory a ride back to the dorm while we get escorted by the dad-looking one.

I shoot her my most disgusted look, but she just nods in agreement, like we're on the same wavelength, like I'm just as disappointed as she is by this turn of events.

And so, as we walk down the main path toward the set of police cruisers, I hold myself back from throttling her silly and take one last look back toward the Hangman. It appears as though the police officer has gone inside to avoid the chilly weather. I stuff my hands into my pockets and am just about to turn back around when I see *him*—the guy I've come to meet. I stop. A weird, tingling sensation runs down the length of my spine, warms up my blood—like fiery pins and needles beneath my skin. I know it's him. I can feel it, can sense it all over me.

He's standing by the side of the building, dressed in darkness, just the tiny, narrow glow of a flashlight beam aimed toward his face. I strain my eyes to make out his features, to try and identify who it is.

"Stacey . . ." Amber calls from the police cruiser. "Hurry up. I need hot cocoa."

I turn to look back at her, to see if she can see him as well. But she's too busy doing that foot-tapping, head-bobbing, chicken-wing dance again to focus on anything.

"Amber—" I murmur, not wanting to say anything more, not wanting to distract the officer's attention from his CB.

"What?" She stops bobbing.

I turn to look back at the side of the building. But this time, no one's there.

fourteen

When we get back to the room, Drea is cuddled up in bed, the phone pressed lovingly against her ear. She laughs at whatever the caller is saying—a huge, bubbly giggle that lights up her face. But then she notices us and her demeanor changes. "Oh, hi," she says in our direction. She sits up and drapes the covers over her bare legs.

"Um, yeah," she says into the receiver. "They're back. Do you want to talk to her?"

She presses the mute button and holds the phone out to me. "It's Chad. He's been calling here all night looking for you."

"Can you tell him I'll call him back?" I sigh, thinking how I can't even remember the last time Chad and I laughed like that.

Drea twists a strand of hair around her finger, the telltale sign that she's about to lie, and then tells Chad that I just ran into the bathroom and will have to call him back. "He's not happy." She clicks the phone off and sits up in bed.

"Yeah, well, he's not the only one," I snap.

"What happened?" Drea asks, seemingly oblivious to my frustration.

"Happened?" Amber pipes up. "Nothing. It was a total bust. Geek-boy Cory closing shop. No one else in sight. We didn't even get a measly scone after hauling our asses over there in, like, fifty-below weather. The best part of the whole evening was meeting this cutie-pie officer who didn't even offer to give us a lift back."

"I saw him," I say, my heart thumping away inside my chest at the mere mention of it—of *him*.

"What are you talking about?" Amber rolls her eyes. "We *both* saw him. Tall, dark, boyishly beautiful."

"Not the officer," I say. "I saw the guy from the boiler room. The one who e-mailed me."

"When? Where?"

"I tried to tell you, but I couldn't with the cop there. On our way to the patrol car, I took a second glance back. He was there."

"What did he look like?" Drea moves to the edge of her bed.

"I don't know. I couldn't really see his face," I say. "It was too dark. And then he was gone."

Amber pulls her makeshift bookmark—a long, thin stick of strawberry taffy—from the middle of one of her textbooks. She peels the wrapper down and stretches off a big chunk. "If you couldn't see his face, then how do you know it was him?"

"I just know. I could feel it."

"Are you sure it wasn't Cory?" Drea asks.

"It couldn't have been," I say. "He and the officer went inside the Hangman as soon as we turned away. This other guy was at the side of the building."

"So, you saw them both go inside?" Drea asks.

"Well, no."

"I don't know," Amber garbles between taffy chews. "I didn't see any of this."

"So? What does that mean—you don't believe me?"

Amber lets out a long and exaggerated sigh. "It just means I wish you would've said something. Maybe we could've done something—distracted the copper, maybe. Now, it's too late."

I slump back on my bed and burrow my face in my covers.

"I told Chad you'd call him right back," Drea reminds me.

I bury my face a little deeper, gathering a thick mound of comforter over my head, imagining myself wearing one of those giant dunce caps. It annoys me that Drea is so obviously concerned about Chad's feelings right now. I mean, I know Chad and I were supposed to talk tonight. I was going to call him after his hockey game to find out how he did, but with everything going on, it must have just zapped from my mind—like not going to Lecklider's detention, and not remembering to finish my English homework, for which I received a big fat zero.

"And your mother called," Drea adds.

Great. I crawl free from the covers and dial Chad's number, readying myself to serve up a hefty dish of apology stew.

"Are you okay?" he asks.

"It's sort of a long story."

"I was hoping to talk to you tonight," he says. "After hockey."

"I know," I say. "I'm sorry. There's just been more weird stuff going on. How was the game, anyway?"

"Wait," he says. "What weird stuff?"

I turn to glance at Drea, hanging on my every word. I get up and peek out our door to see if the common area is free. But, unfortunately, Trish Cabone has camped herself out on the vinyl couch. She smiles when she spots me—a huge, bright, I-just-got-my-teeth-whitened kind of smile. And if that isn't enough, she starts waving her arms around like she hasn't seen me in months.

I respond by closing the door.

"Stacey?" Chad asks.

"Yeah?" I say.

"What weird stuff?" he repeats.

"It was just this weird e-mail from some guy—at least, I'm pretty sure it's a guy. As a matter of fact, I think it might be the same guy who was in our boiler room that night you and PJ stopped by."

I look to Drea, now writing away in her journal, and decide to retreat to the semi-privacy of my bed covers to tell him everything—all about the nightmares and the puking, the e-mail message, the letter postmarked right here in Hanover, and, lastly, about tonight's trip to the Hangman Café.

Chad doesn't say anything, and for several awkward seconds we just sort of hang on the phone, listening to each other breathe.

"Well," I say, finally, "say something."

"Like what?"

"Like, that it'll all work out. That everything will be okay."

"I just can't believe this is happening again," he says.

"Neither can I."

"Do you think there's any way there could be some explanation for all this?" he asks.

"What do you mean?"

"I don't know," he says. "I just think it seems really weird."

"You don't believe me?"

"No, of course I believe you," he says.

"Then what?" I take out my growing aggression on a wad of comforter, squeezing and resqueezing until my knuckles hurt.

"Just what I said, I think it's weird this stuff is happening again. I wouldn't be surprised if it was just somebody's idea of a good time."

"Are you serious?" I flip the covers from my head and sit up straight.

"Stacey, relax," he says.

"Relax? How am I supposed to relax? After everything that's happened, don't you believe I can sense things? Don't you think I'd know if this was all a hoax? I'm puking my *brains* out for god's sake. I'm dreaming about *dead people.*"

"I know," he says, his voice all soft, like he's trying to coax me from a ledge. "I do believe you can sense things, and I know you haven't been feeling well. But a lot's gone on, and being back here, at this time of the year . . . it can't be easy for you."

"I can't believe this," I say. "You sound like the school shrink."

"Stacey—" he pleads.

"I gotta go. I'll talk to you tomorrow." I hang up, feeling completely frustrated and utterly hurt by the sting of his doubt, by his not being able to believe in me . . . when I need so much right now to believe in myself.

"Trouble in paradise?" Amber asks. "I don't know, Stace, you two have seemed pretty bumpy lately . . . and not in a good way."

I look over at Drea, thinking how the tone of my conversation with Chad sounded so much different than hers. She holds the pen tip midair over her diary page, awaiting my response to Amber's comment. But, since I don't feel quite capable of answering to either of them at the moment, I grab the white candle from my night table and press my fingertips against the wax, wanting more than anything to light it, to feel that magical moment my grandmother was talking about, even though the idea of anything remotely magical seems so far away now. I wipe the few stray tears that fall from my eyes, flip the covers back over my head, and pretend to be alone.

fifteen

When Amber and I get to computer class this morning, Mr. Lecklider gives us this long-winded lecture about skipping his detention, finally rewarding us with an even bigger sentence: computer room duty—complete with Windex, wet rags, and mop carts—every day after school next week. Instead of trying to dispute it, I take a seat next to Cory and Emma to resume what feels like our endless group project.

"Wow, that really blows," Emma says, in response to our punishment. She snorts extra hard into her tissue to show her sympathy—a kindly gesture, I suppose.

"Thanks," I say, catching a glance of the designs she's got on her notebook—stupid little hearts with Cory's name in the center, middle-school style.

"Yeah," Cory says, interrupting my bewilderment. "You guys should have come yesterday. Lecklider only kept us for ten minutes."

As if I meant for this to happen. "I forgot," I say.

Cory shrugs and continues to click away at the Web site "we've" developed for class, acting like last night never happened.

Meanwhile, Amber is working Lecklider, trying to get him to buy the excuse that I wasn't feeling well and she was doing her best to nurse me to health. But, judging from Lecklider's posture—completely hunched over in his seat, his back turned so far toward her it almost looks as if she's having a conversation with his butt—it doesn't appear as though she's having any luck.

In an effort to feign group participation, I reach into my backpack and pull out the computer text for the first time this year—even the spine lets out a tiny creaking sound when I open it up to the middle. But what I really want is to get some information out of Cory.

I scoot in extra close, pretending to take interest in the graphics he's working on. "That looks really great," I say, looking down into my book, searching for some keyword that might help me sound even remotely Web literate. "Will we be adding any SQL to this?"

"Huh?"

"SQL? System Query Language?"

Cory's face screws up and so does mine—I can feel it, desperately reading over the bold-faced word in my text, making sure I'm saying it right. Cory turns back to the computer and I end up shutting my book; I was stupid to think it would help me anyway. Instead, I go for the more direct approach: "I hear they're thinking about putting a few computers in the Hangman. Sort of like a cybercafé."

He shrugs and offers up a wry smile, probably detecting the obviousness of that segue.

"How long have you been working there?" I ask.

"Why?"

"Just curious."

He nods, like he already knows why I'm asking. Like he can read my thoughts and knows my suspicions. "It's actually a pretty new gig."

"Was it busy last night?"

He shrugs, that stupid, knowing smile still high on his face.

"So . . . were you working by yourself? Or was someone with you?" I try to sound natural.

He replies by laughing at me—full-blown, belly-jiggling laughter, like he's completely aware of why I'm asking him all these questions, like my efforts at subtlety are just as wasted as his efforts to be normal.

"What's so funny?" I ask. "Was someone working with you or not?"

But he just continues laughing, his tongue pushed forward into the space between his front teeth. And since I'm hardly desperate enough to serve as his entertainment box for even one more second, I wheel my chair away and look to see what Emma's working on—more hearts.

I take a deep breath and silently count to five. It's obviously a waste of time to try and get anything out of Cory. Maybe I'll just have to start hanging around the Hangman more often to see if anything strikes me—to see if that guy comes back. Or maybe Chad's right. Maybe the e-mail message is just part of some joke. Maybe it's the letter that I need to focus on right now. I look up at Amber, who has apparently scored herself a sentence of having to sit beside Lecklider for the remainder of the period and read from a computer manual. Maybe computer room detail isn't so bad after all.

I end up spending the rest of the class finishing up my next period's homework—the *Candide* essay I was supposed to have corrected last night. If I don't start to seriously crack down in my studies, I know I'll end up college-less, which is why, after school, after Lecklider's detention, I end up going straight to the library in lieu of yoga class—actually not such a supreme sacrifice, considering my recent contribution to Savasana.

I ask the librarian for one of the private study rooms in the back, the kind with a door that closes, so I won't be interrupted. And this is where I sit for the next couple hours, slaving away over my list of assignments, skimming through chapters I should have read weeks ago. I even break out my pink and yellow highlighters to mark stuff that sounds important. But that's also the point where I start drawing my own hearts—big and pink and bubbly—hearts that put Emma's to shame.

I wonder what Chad's doing right now. I wonder if he's angry at me after last night's phone call. Maybe he's getting a little sick of all the baggage I seem to carry around.

I flip a page in my lab notes to refocus. That's when I hear a knock at the door. I look up toward the pane of shatter-proof glass that runs vertically beside the door, but there isn't anyone there, just a row of empty study carrels in the distance. A few seconds later the knock comes again.

"Who is it?" I get up from the table and move toward the window, doing my best to try and angle myself so I can see the front of the door. There's another knock. I take a step closer and can just make out the area to the right of the doorknob.

"I'm busy in here," I call through the glass.

But whoever it is knocks again.

"Amber?" I grab the doorknob and whisk the door open. No one. I take a few steps out, into the study area. There are some kids working on a project at one of the round tables to the left, a couple boys working on laptops to the right, and a smattering of other students, lounging in comfy chairs, reading textbook-type stuff.

I look around at the individual faces to see if any of them are watching for my reaction. But, aside from a couple freshmen boys who obviously think I'm newsworthy enough to pause from their riveting calculations, no one seems fazed by me.

I turn around to go back into my study room and feel myself jump. Amber and PJ are standing right behind me.

"Hey, girlfriend," PJ says.

"What do you think you're doing?" I gasp. "You scared the crap out of me."

"Uh, I'd rephrase," PJ says, running his fingers over the electric-blue tips of his purple hair spikes. "I heard about what happened to you in yoga. I'd be super careful about nonchalanting your bodily functions. People just might take you seriously."

"What do you want?" I sigh.

"Why are you acting all wiggy?" PJ asks. "We just came by to shop some books and saw your lazy ass. We thought we'd give a greeting."

"Stacey's been under a little bit of pressure lately," Amber explains to him.

"Dish, please," PJ says.

"There is no dish," I say. "I just don't appreciate people trying to scare me. Why do I keep having to explain that to everyone?"

"Um, a little clarity please," PJ says.

"The knocking," I say. "I'm trying to study."

"What knocking?" Amber asks.

"The knocking—you guys were knocking on the door while I was trying to study."

"No, we weren't," Amber says.

"Right," I say.

"Freaky," PJ says, his eyes widening for extra drama.

"I gotta go," I say.

"Wait," Amber says. "Are you sure you're okay? Do you want us to stay and wait for you?"

"I'm fine," I say, looking around. It's obvious that there are two groups of demons in my life right now—those who are trying to scare me for their own amusement and those who actually might want to cause harm.

I suppose I should wait around for the latter.

"I'll see you guys at dinner." I move back toward the study room door and notice a chunky piece of crystal at my feet. I pick it up. A crystal cluster rock—the kind used for protection, to break through negative energy. The individual crystals that make it up have sort of grown together, healing the jagged pieces, making one solid chunk that fits into my palm.

I squeeze it, concentrating on its energy, feeling a warm surge of vibrations up my arms, over my shoulders, and down my back, practically turning me to putty. It's like I've suddenly been dipped into a bath filled with the silkiest hot-tub water, the bubbling jets pulsating over my skin, massaging my muscles.

I take a deep breath to regain my composure and then look around to see if anyone has noticed all this, including the heat I'm sure must be visible all over my face. I close the study room door and lean back against it to hold myself up, my heart filled with a weird mix of fear and excitement by the mere idea of finding the crystal.

sixteen

After dinner, I come straight back to the room. I pull the crystal cluster rock from my pocket and lay it on the bed in front of me, along with the letter from yesterday. It doesn't make sense that they'd both be from the same person. I consider the possibility that whoever left the crystal might not have known of its protective qualities. But that doesn't make sense either. Crystal cluster rocks are hard to come by—someone would definitely have to go looking for one.

There's a tiny flicker of hope at the back of my mind that the crystal might actually be from Chad, maybe his way of making up for yesterday. I play the scenario out in my mind—Chad stopping by the New Age store on Greenvale Street, asking the person behind the counter for something special, something protective. Only it's not Chad's style to just go leaving something like that at the door. He would definitely have given it to me himself—unless, of course, he thought I was still mad at him.

I pick up the phone to check my messages, to see if he called. Since he wasn't in the cafeteria, I'm thinking he and his teammates just practiced right through their dinner break. I dial the number to retrieve my messages. I have one.

"Hi Stacey," the recording of my mother's voice plays. "It's me. I just wanted to see how you're doing. Did Drea tell you I called last night? I'd really like to talk to you. Call me when you get in. 'Bye."

I click the phone off and slouch down in bed. After a couple minutes of thinking and sulking, I take a deep breath and play my mother's message again. Her voice sounds sort of insistent, like maybe she really has something to talk about. I click the phone back on and dial the number. Something definitely must be up. Usually when my mother calls and Drea answers, she's just as happy to talk to Drea since they're so much alike—since they're both in love with stuff like *Vogue* magazine and Joan & David shoes while I'm whipping up protection spells and casting the ashes out to the wind. Though, I have to admit, after everything that happened last year, it has been better between my mother and me. We talk more; we don't argue as much. And, unlike other years going off to school, this year, when we said our goodbyes, it felt different, harder.

After a few rings, she picks up. "Hi, Mom," I say.

"Stacey, I'm so glad you called."

"What's up?" I ask. "Is something wrong?"

"No," she says. "Nothing. I just wanted to talk to you."

"Oh." I pick Amber's feather pillow off the floor and begin plucking at the quills. "Nothing much is new," I lie. "I have a big English paper due next week, and I haven't even finished the book yet."

"But everything's fine?" she asks. "I mean, you're okay?"

"Yeah," I say, a huge question mark looming over my head.

"That's good," she says. "I just wanted to check."

"Why? Did Drea say something when you called last night?"

"No," she says. "Should she have?"

"No. Everything's fine," I repeat, though I know I'm not fooling anyone. I can hear it in my voice—the wavering in my tone, the guilty squeak of my words.

My mother doesn't respond and I'm thinking it's because she knows what a horrible liar I am. Instead we just sit in awkward phone silence in my bed of lies until I can't stand it anymore.

"I'm having nightmares again," I say.

"What do you mean *again*?"

Is she kidding? When I was having nightmares about Maura four years ago, I told her about them. I told her that

I didn't want to go to sleep anymore, that I was having nightmares every night about the same thing, about the same person; I just never told her who that person was. My mother didn't ask questions. She only responded with mugs of chamomile tea before bed and told me to try and think about more peaceful things before I went off to sleep, like rainbows and starfish.

Then, last year, with Drea, there were more nightmares. And though I wasn't the one to tell my mother about them, when the trial came out, it was pretty much broadcast news. When I was asked at the trial how I knew that Donovan had brought Drea to the forest, I had no other answer but to tell everyone I dreamt it. And so the phone calls began . . . people—strangers—calling me up, asking me if I was having nightmares about them. We ended up having to change our number twice. My mother knows this. Which is why I can't understand how she can ask me what I'm talking about when I say I'm having nightmares again.

"Stacey? Are you still there?"

"Yeah?"

"Well, what do you mean you're having nightmares *again*?"

I really don't feel like going into all of this, playing this stupid game with her when I have no idea why she's playing it at all. Is she still trying to make me into the happy cheerleader daughter that I'm not and never will be? Is she stuck in some sort of twisted denial about who I am?

"Actually, Mom, Drea just came in, and she needs to use the phone. Can I talk to you tomorrow?"

"Sure, honey," she says. "Give me a call, or I'll call you."

"Okay."

"Okay," she repeats. "'Bye."

I hang up, feeling even worse than before. Two lies in one night, and nothing but an impending dose of karma to thank me for it.

seventeen

After the phone call with my mother, I end up studying in my room for about two hours, trying to convince myself that the structure of a neuron—axon, dendrites, and all—is the most riveting material I could possibly be focusing on at the moment. But I'm also waiting for Chad to call. Since it's after nine and I still haven't spoken to him today, I'm wondering if maybe he's holding a grudge. But even if he is, it's still no excuse. He knows I've been under a tremendous amount of stress lately—even if he does believe it's post-traumatic. So,why can't he just put grudges aside and call me like any other good friend would?

After two phone calls to his room with no luck, I end up giving him until exactly 9:15 before I decide to go out. At 9:19, I stuff the crystal cluster rock into my pocket, fill my backpack with a handful of spell ingredients, and make my way out into the night. I think what I really need right now is a little bit of energy cleansing and some definite answers, and I can't think of a better place to find both than outside, under the frost moon—especially since the thought of going down to my altar in the boiler room is so far from appealing right now.

Since the entire campus is surrounded by acres of forest, it isn't difficult to find the ideal space. Despite what happened last year, I still love the forest, especially at night, under the moon and a spattering of stars. The whole atmosphere helps center me, helps me reconnect with the natural spirit and put things into perspective.

Using my small flashlight as a guide, I end up walking around the side of our dorm, across the lawn, and entering the forest by the path that everyone uses when they want to go drinking. I turn to the left and find myself a peaceful spot on the edge—just deep enough to be concealed but not too deep that I can't see the waxing gibbous moon right above me. It's absolutely perfect, just a day from fullness—so amazing that I almost can't believe I spent so long cooped up in my room.

I sit on a patch of grass and do my best to breathe the moon's energy in, to swallow it up and allow the light to soak into my skin. After a few peaceful minutes, I take the crystal from my pocket and place it on the ground in front of me. It can't be a mere coincidence that someone dropped it right outside my study-room door. I know that someone left it for me. I just need to figure out who that someone is before it's too late.

I prop my flashlight up against a rock and begin emptying the spell ingredients from my bag. With a pair of scissors, I start with my hair. I grab one of the longer layers at the side, trim off about four full inches, and then knot the shorn tress at the top to avoid unnecessary frayage. The lock of hair looks weird in my hand, almost surreal, like it isn't really mine. I deposit it into the metal mixing bowl I sometimes use for away-from-home spells and then pour a few droplets of clove oil on top—the normally pale orange liquid now a deep walnut color in such darkness. I move on to my fingernails next. Using a pair of regular nail clippers, I cut them down to the nubs over the bowl, making sure the individual shards drop inside. Then I pour in a few more droplets of the oil, the heavy scent filling the air around me.

I touch the side of my hair where I cut. Despite my careful attempt, I can feel where the chunk is missing, just below my ear. Hopefully the remaining strand is long enough to tie back. If not, I'll just have to do my best at blending. I glance down at my nails, all stubby now; a couple have even started to bleed. I stuff them into my mouth to clot the blood and then plunge them into the mixing bowl. Using my fingers, I mix my hair and bone up in the clove oil, concentrating on the mixture's ability to increase my psychic awareness of self. "Skin and blood, oil and bone," I whisper. "Oh, Moon, I beg thee: Let the truth be known."

I pluck a potato, courtesy of the cafeteria lady on duty this morning, and a black ballpoint pen from the side pocket of my bag. Into the raw potato skin I carve my questions: WILL I KEEP MY PROMISE? and WHAT MIGHT MY PROMISE BE?

I place the potato into the mixing bowl and pour the remainder of the clove oil over it, approximately two tablespoons. I roll the potato in the mixture, making sure it gets moistened, that the carved letters fill up with my spirit.

After several moments of mixing and concentrating, I spread a large sheet of wax paper out on the ground and then pour the mixture onto it, the carved questions facing up toward the moon. I sprinkle some dirt on top, in the form of the letter M, and then roll everything up in the wax paper, securing it with a thick rubber band.

"I offer you, Moon, pieces of myself—my body, my bone—wrapped in love and spirit, and ask thee in return to help me see more clearly, to increase my natural awareness."

Using a spoon, I dig a hole about six inches deep into the patch of soil in front of me, my fingers aching as I struggle to break through the near-frozen earth. I deposit the gift inside, pack the soil back up, and then place the crystal cluster rock over the spot. "Blessed be," I whisper, looking up toward the moon.

The spell complete, I feel completely refreshed, as though suddenly more awake, more attuned with myself and nature. I lean back on my elbows and notice the pine tree just to the side of me. I love pine needles—the way they smell, the smooth and brittle texture when I roll them between my fingers, their ability to protect and dispel negativity. I pick up a couple branches from the ground for later use. That's when I hear a rustling sound coming from a few yards behind me.

I toss the branches into my bag, along with my spell supplies, and grab the crystal. It's probably just some kids looking to booze it up before bedtime. I wait a few seconds for more noise, but I don't hear anything. I switch off my flashlight and stand up. Now I can hear it, the snapping sound of kindling, like someone's made a campfire.

I click my flashlight back on, but keep the beam low, and take a couple steps toward the sound. I can see the bright orangey glow in the distance, the tiny sparks that jump up into the wind. But I don't hear anything else. No voices or laughing. No sounds of beer cans opening or bottles being broken.

The crystal pressed into my palm, I approach the campfire, just a few yards away. I can see a male figure, sitting in a partial clearing laden with rocks, the left side of his body illuminated by the campfire flame. He reaches into his knapsack and begins gathering whatever lies inside into the crook of his arm. He gets up and spreads the objects out around the perimeter of the fire. Rocks, I think. I do my best to try and keep track of how many he's setting down, to see if he's marking all eight directions, north to west. But I can't be sure. He sits back down, pokes at the fire a couple times with a stick, and then pulls something from the side pocket of his knapsack. A jar. He shakes the contents up a few times and then holds the jar up to view. There's a powdery, brownish substance inside, like beach sand, highlighted by the lapping flames. He unscrews the top and then pours something into it from a tiny container. A liquidy substance. He mixes it all up with a stick from the ground, dips his fingers inside, and then rubs the mixture down the side of his face and at the back of his neck.

The whole picture of it, of someone else aside from myself performing some sort of moonlight ritual, completely weirds me out. It's not because I think I'm the only person on the planet who does stuff like this; it's just that, aside from my grandmother and some make-believe witches on TV, I've never actually seen anybody else do stuff like this. And yet, aside from that weirded-out part, there's another part that's intrigued, curious . . . almost hopeful, and I'm not even sure why. I squeeze the crystal, noticing how warm it feels in my hand, how I can't stop shaking.

As curious as I am and as much as I'd like to watch him more, I suddenly feel guilty, as though I'm invading his sacred space, as though the moon is watching me do it. I step backward and point the flashlight beam toward the ground to navigate my way out. There's a group of bushes in front of me. I suck my gut in, hold the slack of my coat, and slip through as cleanly as possible to avoid making any noise. But, on my second step through, I hear a loud, cracking noise. I stop. Look down. It came from the ground. A long, dry branch, cracked in half, my faux Doc Marten pressed down on the broken pieces.

My heart starts beating so hard I think he must hear that too. I click my flashlight off and do my best to hold my breath.

eighteen

I close my eyes and squat as far down into the bushes as my knees will allow.

"Who's there?" he calls, taking a step.

I'm breathing so hard I can barely think straight. I scrunch myself up even further, burrowing my head into my knees, waiting for him to turn around like he's made some mistake.

I can hear him moving toward me, his body shifting through the brush, his footsteps snapping fallen twigs—just a few feet away now.

Still, I don't move. I envision myself as part of these bushes, blending into them, imagining my arms like thick branches, my back like a stump.

He takes another step. And then another. I peek out through my fingers, but I can't see much from this angle; there's just brush, scratching against my face.

"I know you're there," he says, just inches from me now; I can hear the closeness of his voice.

I take a deep breath, muster up the courage of the moon, and straighten up. He's standing right in front of me. I click my flashlight on and shine it toward him. He does the same.

"Stacey?" he says. "What are you doing here?" He stares at me hard, his eyes wide, almost glinting. The color is visible in my flashlight beam, caught somewhere between gray and the lightest blue.

"How do you know me?" I ask, the flashlight shaking in my grip.

There's a mark on his face. From the spell, I presume. A thick and shimmering line down his cheek.

"We've met," he says.

My voice cracks. "Where?"

"Don't you remember?"

I tighten my grip on the flashlight to steady the shake and clench down on my jaw, conjuring up the other night in the boiler room. The guy chasing after me, up the stairs, calling out my name.

"I wouldn't exactly call it *meeting*," I say through gritted teeth.

"What do you mean?"

"Breaking into the boiler room of a girls' dorm in the middle of the night and scaring me half to death is hardly meeting."

"We met before that. Don't you remember?"

I study his face a moment—tawny skin, I think; darkish hair, sort of longish on the top. I try to recollect the voice from my nightmare, the one behind the weathered gray door in the basement, to decipher whether it's the same. But I just can't tell.

"We bumped into each other," he says. "In September, during orientation."

"I don't think so," I say, stepping back.

"Really," he says, moving forward. "I was coming out of the bursar's office. You were hiking up the stairs, two at a time . . ."

It takes me a couple moments, but then I do begin to remember bumping into someone, some faceless person. The avalanche of textbooks out of my backpack and down the stairs, the spill of pencils and other assorted school supplies. I remember being in such a rush, just scrambling there on the ground, trying to pick everything up and cram it back into my bag. Vaguely, I recall somebody trying his best to help me.

"Are you the one who sent me that e-mail?" I ask, changing the subject.

"We need to talk, Stacey," he says.

"Are you the one who gave me this?" I hold the crystal out for show.

"Is that okay?"

"Okay?"

"Yeah," he says. "I wanted you to have it. I was gonna give it to you myself, you know, instead of just leaving it there at the door. But then I saw your friends coming and didn't feel like a party. It was that way at the Hangman, too. I wanted to talk to you alone."

"So we're alone now," I say. And just as soon as I say it, I want to take it all back. I don't want him to know I'm alone. I tighten my hand around the crystal, making a hardened fist, just in case I need to fight.

"I don't want to hurt you, Stacey," he says, as though reading my mind.

"So, what *do* you want?"

"Just like I said; we need to talk."

"So talk."

"Not now. Not here."

"Then I'm outta here." I turn to leave.

"No, don't." He takes another step toward me, his eyes widening.

I shine my flashlight toward the campus grass, just a few yards away, the tall spotlights beaming over the cement benches in the near distance. If I wanted to, I could yell for help and someone would definitely hear me.

"Don't leave," he says. "I do want to talk to you. I'm just in the middle of something right now."

I look over his shoulder at the fire, still alive and kindling, a few stray embers floating up from the heat. "What are you doing?"

"I think you might already have some idea." He looks deeply at me, his slate-blue eyes pouring right into my own, so intense I have to look away. "Can we talk tomorrow?" he asks.

I don't say anything. Because I want to talk to him. Because I want to find out what he has to say. I just don't want him to know I do.

"We could try meeting at the Hangman again," he says. "After hours. But this time you could come alone?"

"Why so late?" I ask.

"Because what I have to say is private. No one else can be around."

"What is it about?"

"You," he says.

"What about me?"

"The crystal I gave you," he begins. "You know what it means, right?"

But instead of answering I focus on the glistening stripe down his cheek—a mix of sandalwood and dandelion, maybe.

"I'll meet you in the library," I say. "In the same study room. Eight o'clock. We can keep the door closed."

"You promise you'll be there?"

"Promise?" I ask, the word so heavy in my mind. "As in, 'will I keep my promise'?"

"Yeah," he says, looking at me funny. "You promise you'll be there?"

I nod, trying to figure him out, trying to decide if he's the one who sent the letter. "But I won't wait for you. At 8:05, I'm gone."

A tiny smile forms on his lips, like he's relieved and pleased at the same time. He pauses a moment to study my face, my chin, my lips. And then locks eyes with me once more.

We stand there a moment in awkward silence—me, not knowing whether or not we're done, if I should leave; him, awaiting my next move. I steal myself from his stare and turn away, back out through the forest, back on relatively safe campus soil. But I can still feel him, his eyes, watching me.

I follow the moon back around to the front of the dorm. Where I'm alone. Where it's safe to let out my breath and untwist the binds on my heart. I lean back against the front door, my heart beating freely now, throbbing inside my chest. My whole body's shaking, the blood stirring inside my veins, over my bones, and beneath the skin. My mind races with questions: *What's wrong with me? Who is this guy? Why didn't I even ask his name?*

I cover my eyes with my hands in an effort to stop the collision of questions, but that only makes me dizzier. Because all I can picture there, in the dark and dankness of my palms, are his penetrating slate-blue eyes.

nineteen

I fumble with my keys at the door of our dorm, trying my hardest to get my fingers to work right, to put the mind-scrambling events of the last twenty minutes far, far behind me. What I need right now is to talk to Chad, to tell him we were stupid to fight on the phone, to recommend that we spend some serious make-up time together.

So what that he didn't call earlier? He was probably busy with his teammates. Maybe he was even thinking that I needed space. I probably did. I just hope he didn't call while I was out because I'm not so sure I can handle lying again tonight, especially to him.

After several attempts, the lock finally clicks and I'm in. I charge my way through the lobby and into the common room. And there he is, sitting on the vinyl couch, a bouquet of wildflowers clenched in his hand, like the perfect boyfriend that he is.

"Look who decided to drop by," he says, standing up.

But instead of saying anything I just run into his arms, melodramatic-style, like right out of one of those old black-and-white movies, the kind where they play lots of orchestral music and the girls wear long, sweepy dresses. Chad hugs me back; his arms encircle my waist, the plastic wrap on the bouquet crinkles against my back.

I peer over his shoulder at Drea, sitting on the edge of the couch, the corners of her mouth turned slightly downward.

"Hi, Dray." I take a slight step back from Chad, but still keep a hand pressed against his shoulder.

She smiles a hello, but then looks away.

"So, where have you been?" He hands me the bouquet of wildflowers. "I've been waiting for you."

"Oh, really?" I ask, looking at Drea, wondering just how long he's been waiting, how long he and Drea have spent together.

"Yeah," Chad says. "But it's no big deal. Me and Drea were just talking about old times." He laughs and looks at Drea, who shares his smile.

"Old times? Like stuff that happened last year?" I ask.

"God, no," Drea says. "*Good* old times. Like stuff from grade school—funny stuff."

"Yeah," Chad says. He proceeds to tell me some story about a middle-school field trip to the zoo and how an elephant squirted Drea with a trunkfull of water. Apparently the water got all over her chest and she was only wearing a thin pink T-shirt. And so their ever-ready teacher pulled this old-lady blouse from her bag of emergency supplies—a blouse with a giant seventies collar, ruffles at the wrists, and pastel zoo animals patterned across the polyester fabric. She made a mortified pre-teen, fashion-savvy Drea wear it for the remainder of the trip.

Drea and Chad laugh at the story like it's the funniest thing ever, but all I'm thinking is how it really isn't that funny at all.

"Well, I'm sorry you had to wait all this time," I say to Chad, putting a blunt end to their ugly-blouse story. "We didn't have plans tonight, did we?"

"No," he says. "It's no big deal. I just thought I'd catch you. You're usually in your room by now."

I look at the clock—11:10. After dorm curfew. "Oh my god, where's Keegan?"

"Relax," Drea says.

"Where is she?"

"Sleeping." Drea gets up and pulls at the length of her flannel pajama-shorts—hiked up, I imagine, for Chad's benefit; pulled back down, I'm sure, for mine. "She had a headache and went to bed early."

I'm starting to feel a smidge of a headache coming over me as well. I rub at the ache in my temples and notice how dirty my fingers are from the spell. I wipe them as discretely as possible on my pants, keeping an eye on Drea's nauseatingly perfect Coppertone legs as she walks back to our room and closes the door behind her.

"Were you at the library tonight?" Chad turns to me.

"I was just out walking," I say, tucking my hair behind my ears so he doesn't notice the missing chunk.

"Walking?"

"Yeah. I went to look at the moon."

"Alone?" he asks.

I nod. I did, after all, go there by myself. "What's the big deal?"

"No big deal," he says. "I guess I'm just surprised, that's all. You've been sort of acting on edge lately. I'd think you'd be leery to go anywhere alone."

"Weren't you the one who said I needed to put the past behind me and get on with my life?" I feel myself getting peeved all over again, and I can hear it in my voice.

"I didn't say it like that, Stacey. And if that's the way it sounded, I'm sorry. I was just worried about you."

"I know," I say, taking a deep breath. "Can we just start over?"

"From where?" he asks.

"The hug." I hold out my arms and Chad wraps me up, relieved, I think, that I'm choosing to keep things in the Land of the Light—where relationships are easy and uncomplicated, where the grave and serious don't have a place.

"Much better." He leans slightly back and moves in for a kiss. And so do I, except I end up tilting my head the wrong way and the kiss lands beside my left nostril.

Chad smiles and squeezes me tighter. I suppose he's right about keeping things simple. This feels so much better, so much easier, the way relationships are supposed to be—all wildflowers and cuddly hugs. Maybe that's what I need right now.

"I hate to go," Chad says, breaking the embrace, "but I probably should. Just in case Keegan gets up."

"We should make plans for tomorrow night," I say. "Something fun. Maybe we could get something to eat off campus. Or go to a movie."

"Definitely," he says. "I'll call you?"

"No," I say. "Let's make definite plans. No more waiting around for phone calls."

"Okay," he says. "How about I drop by here after hockey practice?"

"What time?"

"Eight-thirty?"

"How about nine?" I say. "I'm working on this group project for bio."

"Okay," he smiles. "It's a date."

We spend the next five minutes or so kissing goodbye on the couch, trying to ignore the squeaking sounds of the vinyl as our bodies rub and twist against it. It feels so nice to be this close to him, enfolded in his arms, lip to lip, breath to breath—like normal. Like normal when normal has seemed so far away. I lay my head against his chest and think how great it would be if we could stay like this all night.

But we can't, which is why Chad leaves a few moments later. I walk him to the door, reminding him about our date for tomorrow night, and then retreat back to the room, relieved that everything is finally back the way it should be between us.

twenty

Drea and Amber are still in bed when I wake up the following morning. I roll over to glance at the bouquet of wildflowers Chad gave me—now in a vase with the pine needles I grabbed last night. I smile at it, at the thought of him coming by to surprise me like that.

I pull on my pair of fuzzy peach slippers and stumble out to the pantry for the requisite cup of instant coffee—

barely drinkable but it does the trick. It's absolutely morgue silent. All the doors of the other rooms are closed, as if everyone's decided to sleep in, as if classes are cancelled for the day. I pop a couple slices of bread into the toaster and look out the window toward the parking lot. But everything appears normal—no devastating blizzards to render us all housebound. So where is everybody?

I decide to use their laziness to my full advantage. I gulp down my toast and coffee, grab my shower supplies, and am the first person into the bathroom, making me also one of the few who will actually get to shower with hot water this morning—a rare and delicious treat.

Back in the room, I suit up into my Hillcrest uniform, dab a bit of patchouli oil behind my ears and at the front of my neck, and grab up my books. Drea and Amber are still asleep, the covers pulled up over their ears like they don't want to be disturbed. But instead of honoring their silent request, I snap the window shades open, allowing a surprisingly bright November sun to shine into the room.

"Rise and shine," I say.

Still, no deal—they both look about as rise-and-shining as flatbread. So maybe I'll have to resort to force. I trot right over to their bunks and shake each of them.

"Get up," I say. "You're going to be late." I take another look at my watch; it's 7:45, just a half-hour before the first period attendance bell.

"Mental health day," Amber slurs, rolling over to avoid me.

"I'm not going either," Drea says, following suit.

"Fine." I don't have time to argue unless I want to be late as well. I zip up my coat, pass through the lobby, and make my way out the front door.

That's when I see it. The banner. About twenty feet in length, stretched out across the two cypress trees in front of our dorm, as though just waiting for me.

A swarm of students stands around it. They shake their heads and cover their mouths—Cory and some friend of his, Keegan, Emma, all the girls from our dorm, Mr. Lecklider, Mr. Gunther, Mrs. Halligan, one of the school custodians. Even Donna Tillings. She's dressed in black—from the bowl-like hat with the net that comes down to cover her face to the thick black stockings and square-toed shoes. She looks like she's crying, a smallish bouquet of wildflowers clutched in her hands. They all just stand there, looking at the message and then at me, waiting for my reaction.

But how can I react when I don't even know what to do, when my mind won't accept what it says or what this means? I slowly begin my descent down the dorm stairs, focusing on their faces instead of the words, as though this isn't real, as though the message will change when I reach the bottom.

But it doesn't. I look at it once more, the words stringing together, the message becoming clear:

IN LESS THAN ONE WEEK, STACEY
BROWN, YOU'LL BE BEGGING TO DIE!

I feel a knot in my throat, cutting off my breath. A razor edge slowly slices down my spine. I take a few steps closer toward the banner, my legs, like twigs, ready to snap off beneath me.

"Stacey?"

It's him, the guy from the woods, the one who gave me the crystal. He approaches me from the back of the crowd, a shimmery pearl-colored stripe drawn down the side of his face and those slate-blue eyes, like melted candle wax, burning right into my own.

He uncurls my fist and places a wad of folded paper in the center of my palm—the MASH game. I look down at it, but now it's an origami snake. He closes my hand around it and looks at me for some response. But I can't speak. Can't breathe. And I want to be sick. There's a cold and sticky feeling all around me, in my mouth, clogging up my throat.

He leans into my ear and whispers. "I know how you'll be spending your anniversary."

I open my mouth to scream. Feel myself sit up. Feel the vomit spew out my mouth.

"Stacey!" Drea shouts, rushing out from her bed covers.

"What happened?" Amber jumps down from the top bunk.

But I don't even need to say anything. The answer is dripping down the dresser mirror in the form of A.B.C. bean burrito mixed with long-grain wild rice—the cafeteria's idea of authentic Mexican cuisine. It slides down over the reflection of my face, right in front of me.

twenty-one

I wipe my mouth, flip the bed covers away, and head for the door. Amber and Drea yell out after me, but I have to see for myself. I turn the knob of the main door and run outside into the frosty November morning.

But it's just like normal. No banner. No swarm of students collected around it. Just me—even though it felt so real.

"What's going on?" Drea asks. She and Amber are standing beside me now on the top step—Drea, tying the belt of her robe; Amber, fully outfitted in adult-size Wonder Woman pajamas.

"What do you think's going on?" Amber asks her. "Didn't you catch the exorcist spew on the mirror? She's wigging again. Nightmares, right?"

I nod.

"Lucky for us our beds aren't in front of yours," Amber says.

"Very funny," I say.

"Oh, come on," Amber says, picking a wedge. "We have to look on the bright side of the situation."

"What's going on?" says a voice from behind us. "Are you girls all right?"

It's Keegan. She's standing in the doorway. "I thought I heard an elephant stampede through the common room."

"Is that your way of telling us we need to lose a few?" Amber cinches her gold belt.

"It's my way of asking what's going on," she says.

"Just getting some air," Drea says.

"Yup," Amber agrees. "A little H-2-O for the old windpipes. Don't tell me I didn't learn a couple things in physics class last year."

"Don't you mean Bio-I?" Drea corrects.

"Whatever," Amber says. "They're practically the same class."

"We should go back in," I say.

I brush past Keegan only to find more nosy spectators: Trish Cabone, snot-rag Emma, and some of the other girls on the floor.

"Is everything okay?" Trish asks. She's pulling at her curlicues to give them height, failing to notice the one flat pillow impression on the back of her head.

"Fine," I say. "Just checking the temperature."

It's a ridiculous lie that actually seems to work. Except for Trish and Emma, all the other girls, including Keegan, return to their rooms to savor the few last minutes of sleep before classes.

"We missed you at the chapel service last night," Trish says, not budging from her spot just inches from my face.

I nod an acknowledgment.

"But they're keeping the chapel open all week," she continues. "You know, just in case you wanted to stop by, in case you needed some place to go." She looks back and forth between Drea and me.

"Right now I need to get ready for school," I say. "I can't afford any more detentions."

Emma smiles at us between nose blows, perhaps sensing her roommate's gift of grief giving.

Amber, Drea, and I are just about to file back into our room when I hear a male voice behind me. I whirl around to find Cory and one of his clone friends. Sneakers in hand, Cory hugs Emma goodbye while the clone-friend gives Trish a smooch on the cheek.

"Geek boy?" Amber shouts.

Cory stops and looks back at us. "You didn't see anything, okay?"

"The hell we didn't." Drea folds her arms across her chest.

"For your information, we slept on the floor," the clone-friend says. "We were just cramming for an English exam together."

"Where do I know you from?" Amber asks him.

"I don't know," clone-boy smiles, his left eye twitching. "I've been known to get around." He scratches at the scruff of honey-blond hair on his head and winks at Amber, shooting her with an imaginary pistol.

"Wait." Amber takes a step toward him. "You're the guy from the mailroom. The one who asked me how I'd be spending the anniversary."

"I really don't remember that." He cocks his head to the side, feigning bewilderment.

"You guys should really get going," Trish says, gesturing for Cory and Clone-y to leave. "Our RD is gonna come out here any second."

"Fine," the clone says. "We're leaving." He looks up at us. "It was nice to finally meet you ladies."

"What do you mean 'finally'?" I ask.

"It's just that I've heard so much about all of you."

"Let me guess," Amber sighs, "you're one of the ghost groupies' newest recruits."

"Ghost groupies?"

"Yeah," Amber nods. "That's what I like to call the people around here who can't get any live action, so they go looking for the dead."

"Who says I can't get live action?" clone-boy asks, glancing at Trish.

"If the casket fits," Amber says.

"Let's go," Drea says, tugging at Amber's arm.

Amber pulls away. "What's your name?"

"Hmm," clone-boy says, rubbing at his frizzhead. "That's a tough one."

At that, he and Cory start laughing—stupid, illogical, private-joke laughter, like an instant replay of yesterday in computer class. Trish laughs along as well, but she's still trying to scoot them out.

"Incidentally," Clone says when he can finally contain himself, "how *are* you girls spending your anniversary?"

"Keegan!" Drea shouts, causing them to boot it out the door once and for all.

Keegan emerges from her room. "What? What is it?" she asks.

Emma looks at us, her face at least five shades paler than a few moments ago. She conceals her obvious nervousness with a handful of tissues.

"Nothing," I say, figuring I'm no one to squeal about boyfriends stopping by at the wrong time.

Keegan doesn't say anything else and neither do we. We just go back into our room and lock the door behind us.

"So gross," Amber says, referring to the puke on the mirror. She moves toward it for a closer look. "Did you have Mallowmars last night?"

"Let's not analyze the heave," Drea says. "Let's just get it out of here. Stacey, do you need some Windex?"

But I'm too busy focusing on what's sitting on my bed—
a handheld tape player and an envelope.

"Stacey?" Drea repeats.

The envelope has my name typed on the front, but it
wasn't mailed, and there's no return address.

"What's that?" Drea asks. "How did that get in here?"

I take the envelope with trembling fingers, the vibrations
prickling over my skin—just as real and cold and permeat-
ing as the last time.

"Are you okay?" Drea asks.

I shake my head but rip the letter open anyway. There's
something folded up inside. I take it out—an origami snake.

"That's weird," Amber says.

The origami snake pressed in my palm, I feel a cold,
burning sensation drift up my arms, making my hands
tremble. "I dreamt it," I say. "I felt it—folding paper. In the
common room, the last letter . . . I folded paper."

"What do you mean?" Drea wraps an arm around my
shoulder.

I shake my head. I know I'm not making any sense.

"Look," Amber says, picking up the tape player. "There's
a cassette inside. Should we play it?"

My head is spinning so fast that I don't even answer. I unfold the flaps of paper, doing my best to concentrate on the
action, to sense the message inside. At the same moment
Amber pushes the play button and static-filled music filters
into the room.

"Oh my god," I say, recognizing the tune.

"*Miss Mary Mack, Mack, Mack,*" a child's voice sings from
the player. "*All dressed in black, black, black. She has all but-*

*tons, buttons, buttons straight down her back, back, back. She
cannot read, read, read. She cannot write, write, write. That's
why she smokes, smokes, smokes, her father's pipe, pipe, pipe . . ."*

"Shut it off!" I shout. "Now!"

Drea complies.

"It's the real version," Amber says.

"Who's doing this?" My hand trembles over my mouth.

Drea plucks the half-unfolded origami snake from my
hand and helps me sit down on the bed. "It's going to be all
right." She pushes my hair back off my face, pausing a moment at the shorter chunk at the side where I cut.

"How do you know?" I snap.

She takes a deep breath and finishes unfolding, until the
once tiny origami snake is now a full-blown letter with
tears and creases.

"What is it?" I ask. "What does it say?"

Drea cups a hand over her mouth, allowing the letter to
drop to her lap.

I pick it up. The words stare up at me from the middle of
the page:

IN LESS THAN ONE WEEK, STACEY
BROWN, YOU'LL BE BEGGING TO DIE!

twenty-two

My chest feels like it's about to cave, as if my whole core might collapse in just one breath. Drea pats my back, whispering over and over again how everything will be okay.

"We'll deal," Amber says. She pries the letter from my hands, tosses it out of sight, and then shimmies over to the open window to stick her head out. "I don't see anything." She closes it back up and locks it.

"Why wasn't it locked in the first place?" I ask.

"I'm pretty sure it was," Amber says. "Not like that matters. If someone wants to get in, they will."

"Maybe they didn't break in through the window," Drea says. "Maybe it was somebody who lives here. I didn't lock the door on the way out."

"Well, then, why was the window open?" Amber asks. "It wasn't open before."

"It doesn't make sense," I say. "It doesn't make sense that someone would be keeping such close tabs on us that they would know it the moment we all stepped out of the room. That they would be able to open the window, climb in, leave stuff, and then climb out before any of us came back. Plus, how would whoever it is know which bed is mine?"

"I don't know, Stacey," Amber says, glancing toward my night table. "If the crystal and bowl of dried herb thingies didn't tip them off, maybe it was the shrine of candles, those weird cone pieces, or that Bunson burner mechanism you have there."

"The cone pieces are incense," I say. "And that's a clay burner for lighting them."

"A serious must-have," Amber says.

"Okay, so maybe it isn't so hard to tell which bed is mine."

"Well, there's certainly no mistaking which bed is *mine*." Amber grabs the bright pink boa hanging from her headboard. She drapes it over her shoulders and then turns to gaze over at Drea's bed. "Your bed is looking a bit stark lately, Dray. Is that what happens in a drought?"

"Better a drought than your monsoon of a reputation," Drea says.

"Can we just stop with the jokes for five minutes?" I ask.

"Who's joking?" Amber asks.

"That's not Maura's voice on the tape, is it?" Drea asks, deciding to ignore Amber.

I shake my head.

"I didn't think so," she says. "It sounds too much like an actual recording. Like an actual children's CD that you could go out and buy."

"Yeah," Amber agrees, "but taped off another cassette or CD or something because of the static and the music in the background." She pushes the Eject button and pops the tape out.

"What is it?" I ask, noticing how her lips have twisted up like she just failed a test.

Amber angles the cassette toward me, the words on the label staring back at me: I'M WATCHING YOU.

"It doesn't mean anything," Drea says. She's shaking her head, pressing her fingers into her temples, wanting more than anything, I think, to believe that herself.

"It means I'm being watched."

"Wasn't 'I'm watching you' Donovan's catch phrase last year?" Amber asks.

"Exactly," Drea says. "And look at the lettering. It's also like last year—the uppercase red. It could just be some copy-cat prankster. You know? One of the ghost groupies . . ."

"Could be," Amber says. "Though 'I'm watching you' is pretty EOE."

"EOE?" I ask.

"Yeah, you know, an equal opportunity expression. It's pretty generic. It could just be a coincidence. Especially since I'm so done calling this a prank."

"So am I." I swallow hard and look at Amber, hoping for one of her stupid jokes, waiting for Drea to tell me that everything will be fine. But it just remains quiet among us for several seconds.

Finally, Amber feeds the cassette back into the player and hits fast forward a bunch of times, followed by the play button. "Nothing," she says. She flips the tape over and tries that side as well. "It's blank except for that one song."

I take the tape out and press it between my palms, trying my best to concentrate, to sense something. "The letter *M*," I say, picturing it pressed behind my eyes. "Like the first time I dreamt about it."

"Now, would that be *M* for Maura or *M* for murder?" Amber asks. "Or maybe it's *M* for the 'Miss Mary Mack' song." She over-enunciates the *M*s on the title. "I'm a wee bit drained of all this rainy-day clue stuff, Stacey."

"What are you talking about?"

"Your insights," she says. "They're all so foggy."

"This isn't exactly easy for me."

"It isn't easy for any of us," Drea says.

"I know," I say, draping my arm around Drea, noticing how watery her eyes look.

She wipes the tears that dribble from the corners of her eyes and takes a deep breath. "I'm okay."

"Are you sure?" I ask. "Maybe Amber and I should talk about this someplace else."

"No," Drea says, sitting up to straighten her posture. "I want to help. We need to figure this stuff out, like, why an origami snake?"

"It was in my dream," I say, remembering the detail. "I also sensed it."

"You sensed origami snakes?" Amber winds the boa around her head, turban-style.

"Well, not exactly," I correct. "When I got that first weird letter, I was able to sense paper folding."

"Are you sure it wasn't paper rolling?" Amber asks.

"Hilarious," I say.

"Yeah, but why a snake?" Drea asks, ignoring Amber. "Why not a rat or a goat? And why that 'Miss Mary Mack' song?"

"That's easy," Amber says. "Because when Stacey fell asleep in yoga class she started singing some twisted version of it."

"And now I have everyone singing that stupid little tune at me." I sigh. "That and throwing barf bags in my path."

"Mortifying," Amber says.

"Were you dreaming about Maura this time as well?" Drea asks.

"No," I say. "My nightmare this morning was different." I grab a couple paper towels and a bottle of Windex and begin mopping up the mirror. Between wipes, I tell them all about the banner and the students gathered around it, and then segue into my little run-in with the guy from the woods. I tell them how he was the one who sent me that e-mail and broke into the boiler room.

"He's also the one who handed me the origami snake in my dream," I say. "He wants me to meet him later."

"We're so there!" Amber declares. "What time?"

"No," I say. "I think I should go alone. He wants to talk to me alone."

"Are you crazy?" Drea asks.

"No one's going anywhere alone," Amber says. "Not for a good two weeks."

"No," I say, scavenging through my spell drawer for a bottle of cinnamon oil. "I'll be fine." I dab my finger with a bit of the oil and then touch all four corners of the mirror to help restore positive energy. "Plus," I continue, "he'll know if you guys are with me. He's obviously watching me."

"Wait," Drea says. "Is he the one who's sending you all this stuff?"

"Obviously," Amber says. "The guy's a total psycho."

"Actually, I don't know who this stuff is from. I need to talk to him about that. But I'm thinking it's from someone else."

"Why?" Amber asks, fake-smoking one of the feathers from her boa.

I glance back at the crystal on my night table, wondering if I should explain about its healing qualities, how the person who gave it to me couldn't possibly be the same person to send me something so menacing. But then I change my mind, considering how ridiculous the words sound in my head—how ridiculous it would be to try and explain such a theory when breaking into the dorm's boiler room in the middle of the night is nothing less than menacing. When the guy who gave me the crystal was in fact the same person who handed me the origami snake in my nightmare.

"Look," I say, "I need to go alone. I can't waste any time here. I only have a week."

"Less than a week," Drea says, nibbling at an acrylic nail.

I nod, swallowing down the lump of fear in my throat. "I'll call you guys as soon as I'm done talking to him. But I can't afford having you around, having him see you. Deal?"

Amber grits her teeth. She purposefully plucks a handful of feathers from her boa and throws them to the floor, as if they could smash. "So pluckin' bunk," she says.

"I'm sorry," I say. "But I don't see where I have another choice here."

"There's always a choice," Amber says, retreating to her bed.

"We just don't want anything to happen to you," Drea says. "I mean, if you were to go there alone, and something bad happened, how do you think we'd ever be able to forgive ourselves?" Drea bites down so hard on one of her acrylic nails that it makes a loud cracking sound, but still, it doesn't seem to faze her. She shakes her head and covers over her mouth, as if she could fall apart at any moment.

"I don't know," I say, looking down at my amethyst ring. All I know is that right now I have to worry about myself, especially since there's no point in denying it further. The danger that's coming in less than one week is definitely pointed at me.

twenty-three

I make a genuine attempt to concentrate in school. I bring all my books, arrive to all my classes on time, and even try my best to listen to what the teachers are saying instead of focusing on the area above their heads, drifting off into space. But, with everything going on in my world, I just can't stop thinking about tonight—about meeting the guy from the woods, finding out as much as I can, and seeing if any of it helps to piece the details of my nightmares into some sort of place.

I just hope I can squeeze all of that into the hour window I have open before I'm supposed to go meet Chad. I would postpone our date for tonight, even move it back a half-hour or so, but with all the negative energy stacked up between us lately, I've decided we can't afford to put off our much-needed alone time for even five measly minutes.

So, after entire lunch and dinner sessions spent trying to convince Drea, Amber, and PJ to make themselves scarce while I go meet Mystery Boy, I'm thinking things are pretty much a go—that is, until the dinner conversation takes an unexpected turn.

"Are you at least going to tell Chad you're going?" Drea asks.

"I hadn't exactly planned on it," I say.

"I think he should know," Drea says.

"I could tell him," PJ says. "I've been known to swing by the hockey rink during practice, you know, to offer the boys a pointer or two."

"Let's face it," Amber says, "you don't exactly have much of a pointer to offer." Amber raises her pinky finger at him, wiggling it slightly as she sips from her juice box.

PJ fork-flings a glob of mashed potatoes in retaliation, but, instead of hitting her, it hits Donna Tillings, sitting at the empty table behind ours. She turns to us, the dark circles under her eyes highlighted by the blanched color of her skin.

"Oh, sorry," PJ says, lowering his fork. "Bad aim."

Donna's lips part—chalky-white lips with dots of red where they've obviously been bleeding. She nods slightly, her gaze dropping toward the floor, and then she turns around to resume her dinner.

"Freak show," Amber mouths.

"No," I whisper, remembering how Donna made an appearance in my nightmare last night. "It's kind of sad the way she's changed so much."

"I agree with Amber," PJ whispers. "It's total freak show. I mean, yeah, your best friend croaks . . . it sucks goat cheese big time. But why should that make you turn into some zombie girl? Life goes on. You know what I mean?"

"Have *you* ever had a best friend die?" I hiss.

He shakes his head.

"Well, come talk to me when you do."

The table goes library silent.

"What time are you supposed to meet him tonight?" Amber asks after a weighty pause.

"Eight. And like I said, I'm not telling anyone about it. End of story."

"Except for us," Amber corrects.

"I still think Chad would want to know," Drea says.

"I disagree."

"How can you say that?" Drea asks. "He cares about you."

"I know he does. And, yeah, I think in theory he'd want to know if I was in any kind of danger."

"You *think*?"

"Okay, I know. But I also know he'd think something like this was someone's idea of a joke, that I should tell the administration or campus police about what's been happening, and that Veronica Leeman's appearances in my dreams only cement the fact that I'm post-traumatic-stressing after last year."

"Maybe you're not giving him enough credit," Drea says.

"You're not going to tell him," I say.

"What if he calls?" she asks.

"He won't," I say. "He'll be at practice until he comes to pick me up."

"But what if?" she asks. "And you aren't back yet?"

"Tell him I just stepped out for a sec."

Drea shakes her head to show her disapproval and resumes pushing her food around on the plate. I hate asking her to lie for me. But I'd hate it more if Chad and I got into another fight.

twenty-four

I arrive at the library at promptly 7:45—enough time to get settled, have him see that I am indeed by myself, and, most importantly, to run through the list of questions in my head so I don't leave any out. I'm hoping this won't take too long since I'm still supposed to be meeting Chad at nine back at the dorm. But just in case, I've stocked Drea up with more of my lies. If Chad arrives to pick me up before I get back, she's going to tell him that I'm finishing up a last-minute group project in the library and will be back ASAP.

I close the study room door behind me and take a seat at the table to wait. The crystal cluster rock rests in my pocket. I take it out and focus on the broken edges, now healed over with smooth slabs of glasslike crystal. I wonder how long the healing process took and what inspired the transformation, why it didn't instead break up into a million tiny fragments.

After several minutes of waiting, I find myself rapping my fingertips against the smooth mahogany tabletop, just staring at the blank white wall in front of me, at a pair of houseflies lingering there. I imagine them as Amber and Drea—the two doing everything they can, including self-mutating spells, to make sure I'm not alone.

I smile at the thought and then peek at my watch. It's 8:07, my cue to leave. I stuff the crystal back into my pocket and get up from the table. That's when the doorknob twists open and he comes in. He closes the door behind him and just stands there, staring right at me, those slate-blue eyes even more lucid under the fluorescent lights.

"You're late," I manage. "I was just gonna go."

"I got caught up in some stuff," he says, looking toward the table. "Do you want to sit?"

We take our seats across from one another. "So?" I say. "What's all this about?"

"You," he says.

"Me?"

He nods.

"What about me?"

He looks down at his fingers, as though not quite ready to tell me. His hands are bony but strong, the individual muscles outlined in smooth, olive skin. "It's kind of hard to say," he begins, "since we barely even know each other."

"Just say it," I tell him. "I've waited long enough."

"Could we maybe just talk a bit first?" he asks. "Get to know each other a little? You don't even know what my name is, do you?"

"What's your name?" I ask.

"Jacob."

"Okay, then, Jacob, what do you have to tell me?"

"Were you maybe wondering what I was doing in the woods last night?" He locks his eyes on mine, forcing me to look somewhere—anywhere—else. I focus on his chin and the contour of his cheeks, the way the angles of his face square off at a strong, defined jaw line.

"Maybe a little," I say, looking away entirely.

"Maybe you already know." He scoots in closer, enabling me to smell him. He smells like wheat grass and candle wax.

"Are you going to tell me?" I ask, leaning back, hooking my feet around the legs of my chair.

"I want *you* to tell me," he says.

I take a deep breath and remind myself why I'm here— how he might be able to help me, how it's possible he could offer some bit of information that would help glue the pieces of this puzzle together. "Are you the one who's been leaving me stuff?" I ask.

"What stuff?"

"The letters and the cassette," I say, somewhat reluctantly. "And the message on the window in the boiler room of my dorm."

He shakes his head.

"But you know who did," I say, more of a statement than a question.

"No."

"Then what?" I ask. "What am I doing here?"

"I think you already know the answer to that. Don't you?" He leans in closer and looks at me hard, his eyes almost challenging me.

"I think I've wasted enough time," I say, my voice cracking over the words. I get up from the table and make my way to the door.

"Who's Maura?" he asks, just before I have the chance to turn the knob. "And why is she haunting your nightmares?"

I turn back around. "What did you just say?"

"I think you heard me."

"How do you know about that?"

"I know a lot about you, Stacey."

I plunk back down on the seat across from him. "You obviously heard about the trial last year. How I told everyone about my experience with nightmares."

"I'm talking about the nightmares you're having about Maura *now*," he says.

I feel my chin tremble. I'm not sure what to say or how to respond.

"You're having nightmares about Veronica Leeman as well," he continues. "You're scared you'll end up just like her. That's why you dream about her, you know. She represents death for you."

How does he know these things? Did Amber or Drea let it leak out? Did PJ? I think back to the nightmare I had about Veronica Leeman, how all the girls on the floor gathered around, including Trish Cabone, who asked me about it later.

"Who told you about that?" I ask.

"No one told me," he says. "No one had to."

"What do you mean *no one*?"

"I mean, I'm having nightmares about *you*, Stacey."

twenty-five

It takes me a couple seconds to regain my breath. Jacob is staring at me intensely, awaiting my response. But I'm not sure where to begin. I look down into my hands to avoid his gaze. "What kind of nightmares?" I ask, finally.

"Like the ones you have. Like the kind you had about Maura before she died. Like the ones last year, with Drea."

I bite my lip to stop the trembling. Everything he's saying is just so hard to swallow. He doesn't even know me, and yet he seems to know so much about me.

"What happens when you dream?" I ask.

"What do you mean?"

"I mean, does anything happen to you?"

"Happen? Like what?"

I continue to stare into my hands as though they hold all the answers. I'm not sure there's a nonchalant sort of way to ask him if his nightmares cause freakish side effects like bedwetting or puking, so I just shrug it off.

"I'm more like you than you think," he says.

"What do you mean?"

"I mean I can see things in my dreams."

"And what have you seen?" I ask, feeling myself swallow.

But instead of telling me outright, he takes his time and starts from the very beginning. He tells me that sometime at the end of last year, just before summer vacation, he started having nightmares about me—only he didn't know who I was. He didn't know where I lived, or what my name was, or if I was just a figment of his dreams. But the nightmares became more intense, more telling, revealing to him where I went to school. And so he started doing the research, which supposedly led him to the details of last year. He claims he then got a gnawing urge to transfer to Hillcrest from his private school in Colorado.

"And your parents didn't mind?" I ask.

He shrugs. "Yeah, I mean, they were against it at first, but then they kind of got used to the idea."

"Why? That doesn't make sense."

"Because I'm different from them. And maybe they're a little bit tired of that. I think it was almost easy for them to send me across the country—convenient. I think maybe they hope I'll come back as some soccer jock or prom king. Maybe they think some all-inspiring teacher can make me stand on a desk or listen to Mozart—transform me into the next dead-poet-loving-society member."

I nod, knowing full well what he means.

"All I know is that I had to follow what my nightmares were warning me," he continues. "Regardless of what my parents wanted. I've had stuff like this happen to me before—nightmares, I mean. Maybe not as intense as this, but still they came true. I just wouldn't have been able to forgive myself if something happened to you and I did nothing to try and stop it. Even though I didn't know who you were . . . I know it sounds crazy, but I had to do something. I had to try and find you."

It's quiet between us for several moments. It's all I can do to remain seated, to not topple off my chair or go running out of the room. It just doesn't make sense. How we could be so similar.

I look back at him, wondering if he's being genuine, if I can even trust him. My heart is beating so fast just imagining the possibility of his honesty, the idea that someone could relate to me this way.

"When you got here," I begin, "how did you know who I was? How were you able to tell I was the girl you'd been dreaming about?"

"I knew it when we bumped into each other that day. I could sense it." He swallows. "All over me."

I swallow, too.

"Do you know what that feels like?" he asks. "To sense things so intensely that your blood almost feels like it could boil right out of the veins?"

I can almost feel it now. I clasp my hands and purse my lips, trying to hold it all in place, to remain in control. "So?" I say, finally.

"So," he says, "now that I'm here, my nightmares have been stronger than ever."

"And what do they reveal?"

He looks away like he doesn't want to tell me.

"I have to know," I say. "What do you see?"

"I see you," he says, unclasping my hands and taking one in his own. He rubs it gently with his thumb, causing the blood in my veins to boil up and bubble right over my bones. "Lying in a casket."

twenty-six

Before we say our goodbyes, Jacob scribbles his number on a slip of paper and tells me to call him if I need anything. But what I really need right now is to call Drea and Amber—to tell them I'm okay. I rush down to the phone in the lobby.

"Where have you been?" Drea asks.

"What do you mean? I've been here—in the library."

"I called the library. I had you paged."

"I didn't hear any page," I say.

"Me and Amber have been completely freaked," she says. "Amber nabbed PJ from his room. They're on their way to the library now to look for you."

"I'm fine," I say.

"So, you met him?" Drea says. "He was there?"

"Yeah."

"And?"

"And we should talk about it. But later. Not here." I glance around the lobby. There's a spattering of students checking out books at the front desk and hanging out by the door.

"Chad came by around quarter of nine to pick you up," Drea says.

I look at the clock. It's 9:20. "Oh my god," I say. "Was he mad? What did you tell him?"

"He was more frustrated than mad," she says. "He waited for, like, half an hour, but then took off. I told him you were working on a group project, but I'm not sure he bought it."

"I should call him now," I say. I look toward the door just as Amber and PJ bust in.

"Oh my god," Amber says, a big fat salami stick tucked under her arm. "Thank god you're okay. I was totally wigging."

"What is that?" I ask, pointing at the two-foot-long stalk of cured meat.

"My weapon," she says, battering up as though at home plate.

"Yeah," PJ says, pulling a water pistol from his jacket pocket. "We've come to save you."

"I gotta go," I tell Drea. "The cavalry has arrived." I hang up and go to dial Chad's number.

"*Très rude,*" PJ says, grabbing the receiver and hanging up. "We come all the way down here to save your sorry self and this is how you repay us? Making phone calls on *our* time?" He squirts a couple times into his mouth with the water pistol—a bluish-green liquid.

"We should go," I say. "We'll talk about this later."

"So you talked to him?" Amber says, peeling at the wrapper on her meat stick. "Details, please."

"Later," I insist.

Amber sighs but she doesn't object. I grab both her and PJ by the arm as I make my way toward the exit doors, but, unfortunately, we're stopped by Cory before we can even make it out. He's with his friend, the guy who stayed over at our dorm last night.

"What finds you ladies here on a Friday night?" Cory asks us.

"Unfortunately, your ugly ass," PJ says.

Cory's friend ignores PJ and leers directly at me. "Let's hear it, Stacey, what kind of hexes are you casting up tonight?"

"Ones that make your boyhood shrivel up," Amber says, holding up the wrinkly meat stick as an example. "Care to be the first?"

"Yeah!" PJ says, taking position behind Amber, his water pistol aimed and ready for battle.

"Seriously, now," Cory's friend continues at me. "Let's hang out. Let's do something crazy: drink someone's blood, sacrifice a couple lambs . . . I know this really great farm not too far from here."

"I'm afraid you're talking to the wrong person," I say, pushing past him and Cory, now cackling back and forth.

"My name's Tobias, by the way," Cory's friend says. "I'm new here."

"Why couldn't you tell us that yesterday?" I ask.

"Didn't feel like it," he says. "Wanted to remain enigmatic."

"More like ignoramus," I say, stopping to check what's keeping Amber and PJ. PJ has managed to let all the bluish liquid leak out of his water pistol and onto the floor. Amber is helping him wipe it up with a clump of her bra stuffing before the librarian sees.

"I think we could brew up some really nifty concoctions together," Tobias continues, his left eye twitching at me.

"Let's go!" I call to Amber and PJ, ignoring Tobias' suggestion.

"Tell me, Stacey," Tobias interrupts, "do all witches pee their pants and throw up in yoga class? Or is it just the ones who suck at saving people?"

I freeze but feel my mouth drop open. I look at him, at the big, stupid grin on his face.

"Tsk, tsk, Stacey," he says. "Should have been at Veronica Leeman's chapel service. Not very respectful of the dead, are you?"

"Screw you," Amber says to him. She grabs me by the hand and whisks me through the second set of doors.

Tobias follows us out. "I'm only looking out for Veronica's best interest, Stacey. And she wants you gone."

"What are you talking about?" Amber turns to him.

"We've talked to her."

"Must have been a pretty one-sided conversation," Amber says. "In case you've forgotten, the girl is dead."

"We've talked to her spirit," Cory calls after us, as we walk away. "And she's mad as hell."

twenty-seven

I try calling Chad as soon as I get back to the room, but he doesn't pick up, even after seven consecutive attempts. Great! I contemplate making the hike across campus to his dorm, but since I really don't feel like leaving the security of my bed and my medicinal bowl of lavender pellets right now, and since he obviously doesn't want to talk to me, I decide to just leave a couple messages and hope for the best. I feel really bad that I missed our date, but my love life isn't exactly my top priority right now—it can't be. Nor can I afford to preoccupy myself by worrying about Cory and his so-called séance. I need to focus on myself, on the prospects of ending up in a casket before the week is up.

I tell Drea and Amber all about my meeting with Jacob, every single detail, from crystal cluster rock to coffin. Minus, of course, the part about his eyes and the way he touched my hand, and the stupid, *stupid* way I feel all jittery around him.

"So, what's that supposed to mean?" Amber asks. "That he's some warlock? Are you seriously buying that dung?"

"Not a warlock," I say, "a witch. Warlocks are people who break oaths." It's weird to even give him a label, to stamp some ready-made definition to his forehead so others can try to comprehend him.

"Whatever," Drea says. "A guy witch?"

"It's not a gendered religion," I say. "And you don't have to be female to sense things."

"I suppose a guy witch *could* be kind of sexy," Amber says, rubbing at her chin in thought. "But that still proves squat. Everybody at this sad-ass campus knows about your Maura nightmares. You talked about them at the trial last year, when they asked you about your first experiences with premonitions."

"I know," I say, mashing the lavender pellets up with my thumb, soaking up the soothing scent. "But when I talked about the Maura nightmares then, I was referring to the ones I was having three years before. This is different. He knows I'm having nightmares about her *now*. He also knows I'm having nightmares about Veronica Leeman."

"So, who else besides us knows that stuff?" Amber asks.

"Just you guys," I say.

"And Chad and PJ," Drea adds.

I nod.

"So they totally could have dished about it," Amber says. "Especially PJ."

"I guess," I say. "But why would Jacob come all the way here from Colorado to find me and tell me I'm in danger? What would he have to gain?"

"Maybe he's one of the ghost groupies," Amber says.

"You don't think there's any chance he could be telling the truth about the premonitions?" I ask.

"We don't even know if he's telling the truth about transferring here from Colorado," Amber says. "For all we know, he could be from the next town over."

"Of course there's a chance," Drea interrupts. "Look at Stacey. Look at how she's able to predict stuff."

"Yeah, I guess it's possible," Amber says. "It just seems pretty sketchy, you know? Like he's trying too hard to get on Stacey's good side. I just think we really need to be sure."

"I guess," I say. "I guess we should probably try to find out if he really *is* from Colorado, and then ask PJ and Chad if they've said anything."

"I don't think Chad would go spreading stuff," Drea says.

"You're right," I say. "He wouldn't. Especially since he seems to think my nightmares are all psychosomatic."

"*Psycho* being the operative word," Amber says.

"It just makes a lot sense to me," I say ignoring Amber's comment, "why someone would travel to such great lengths to forewarn a person that their life is in danger . . . Sort of a way to safeguard yourself from years of impending guilt."

"Yeah, but then why did he wait so long to contact you?" Drea asks. "I mean, if he's supposedly been having nightmares about you since the summer . . ."

"Good question" I say, biting down on my lip.

"For now, I think you should stay away from this guy," Amber says. "For all you know, he could be another Cory clone."

"I don't know," Drea says. "Maybe he could really help us. I mean, let's say he really *is* from Colorado—why would he bother traveling all this way if he wasn't telling the truth? Do you think anyone's that fanatical?"

"Look at freak-show Trish Cabone," Amber says. "She came here all the way from Rhode Island."

"Um, that's only like a state away," Drea says. "When was the last time *you* looked at a map?"

Amber shrugs.

"Maybe he came here for the prestigious Hillcrest name," Drea says.

"Yeah," Amber says, "I'm sure all the Ivies are psyched to get applicants from Kill-crest Prep."

"Look," I begin. "All I know is I'm having nightmares that tell me that I'm going to be begging to die in less than a week. I'm getting letters that say the same thing. And meanwhile, some guy is claiming to be dreaming about my funeral."

"Don't forget middle-of-the-night boiler room visits, evil children's music, and red letter *M*s," Amber says.

"Right," I say. "I'm thinking I should take it all seriously."

"*Very* seriously," Drea says.

Amber grabs a pinch of lavender pellets and drops them down the front of her shirt. "I think we should keep an eye on Cory and Tobias as well."

"And Trish and Emma," Drea adds.

"Do you think there's any truth to their lame-ass séance?" Amber asks.

"What are you talking about?" Drea asks. "What séance?"

"Apparently Cory and his ghost-groupie clones have conjured up Veronica's spirit," Amber says. "They say she's piss-mad at Stacey."

"Try not to stress about it," I say. "I mean, I know it's easier said, but I'm with Amber on this: their séance is definitely lame."

"How do you know?" Drea takes a deep breath and grabs a bar of chocolate off her night table. "I don't think I'm ready for this."

"We'll deal," Amber says.

"Famous last words," Drea says, gnawing away at the block of chocolate comfort.

twenty-eight

I lie awake in my bed, trying to go over and over and over in my head what my mind and body are trying to warn me about, how the messages and the song play into that, as well as everything that Jacob said. But instead of becoming clearer, I only feel more confused, more funkified, like my head is a giant bingo tank and the endless questions that spin around inside are the rotating bingo balls. I just can't seem to focus longer than two whole minutes. It seems that every time I try, my mind begins to wander. As much as I want to, I just can't stop thinking about Jacob, which completely infuriates me because I'm thinking about him and not about Chad. And what infuriates me even more is that I shouldn't be thinking about either of them. I should be trying to figure everything out.

Which is why I decide to do a spell tonight, one that promotes clarity, one that will help me gain a better understanding of things. I set the family scrapbook open atop my bed for inspiration and reference, and I go ahead and make copies of the letters at the library, just in case I need them as evidence later. I place the copies in my jewelry box for safekeeping and keep the originals for the spell.

Amber and Drea agree to help me. They sit at the foot of my bed—Amber, busy charging up all the spell supplies by passing them one by one through the incense smoke, and Drea, cutting the letters up into tiny squares.

It feels good that Drea is helping me like this, talking about the situation as if it's our problem and not just mine. I know how hard this must be for her, not only putting aside any negative energy between us but putting my needs well above her own.

Using a razor blade, I carve into the top of a thick yellow candle, doing my best to get close to the wick, but not to sever it, and to dig a deep enough bowl-like space for melted wax to collect. I light the candle and place it on a ceramic plate. I need to capture Jacob's essence in some way. Normally, I'd use a lock of his hair or a fingernail shard, as the family scrapbook suggests, but since I don't have those things I need to be resourceful. The crystal comes to mind. I palm it, wondering if I could make it work, but it really doesn't capture him—his spirit—the way I need it to. I need something more personal, more intimate. I rack my brain for some idea, but the only one that comes to mind, the one that I can't seem to shake, is that slate-blue eye color and the way those eyes made me feel, making me almost want to gouge out my own eyes with a ballpoint pen. I mean, *what* is wrong with me? Still, since it's the only thing that I can think of right now, I have no choice. I ignite my lightest blue candle and place it to the side.

"So," Amber begins, "did this Jacob guy admit to sending you these letters?"

"No," I say. "It was weird. He seemed to know about the stuff I was getting, but then when I asked if it was from him, he just shook his head."

"So, if it isn't him," Drea says, "then it could be anyone."

"Freakin' brilliant, Sherlock," Amber says.

"No, I mean, it could be *anyone*. Even a girl. We were originally thinking it was a guy, right? Because of the break-in. Because Stacey heard a male voice and saw a male figure that night in the boiler room. But if that was Jacob, and if it was Jacob who sent the e-mail, then we have no other evidence that it's a guy who's after her, right?"

"Tell me, O wise one," Amber intones, "if you were a crazy stalker, would you really admit to your target that you were the one who was sending her all this psycho threatening stuff?"

"If I was a crazy stalker," Drea says, "I wouldn't even admit to *knowing* about the psycho threatening stuff."

A good point. Which is why I believed Jacob when he said the messages and the cassette weren't from him.

"You think a girl sent these letters?" Amber asks, running the spool of black thread through the incense smoke.

"It's possible," Drea says. "I mean, it doesn't necessarily have to be a guy."

"No way," Amber says. "These letters are so Y-chromosome. A girl's death threats would have way more style."

"There's a brilliant theory." Drea cuts up the last of the letters and drops the tiny paper squares into a bowl. "We really shouldn't rule anyone out."

"And we won't," I say, pouring the bowl of melted yellow wax into a ceramic dish. I drip the melted baby-blue wax onto it and then swirl the two colors together with the back end of a mixing spoon—yellow for clarity and blue to represent Jacob.

After the wax has had ample time to cool, I grab it up in my fingers and sculpt it into the shape of a body.

"What is that?" Amber asks.

"An effigy," I say, rubbing the warm and buttery wax between my fingertips.

"A what-a-gy?" Amber asks.

"An effigy," I repeat. "A wax figure, basically."

"Like voodoo?" Drea asks.

"Sort of," I say. "It will help make things more clear." I unravel several feet of thread from the spool and wrap it around the effigy's waist as many times as I think is necessary, until I feel in my heart I've gained full control of it. Then I continue to work the thread around the figure— over the shoulders, through the legs, and around the ankles, concentrating on the idea of harnessing my confusion and overcoming it.

"Do you think he likes that?" Amber asks.

"Do I think *who* likes *what*?" I ask.

"Effy," she says, giving my wax figure a name. "Do you think he enjoys being tied up like that? You know, like a turn-on?"

"Someone get her some help," Drea sighs.

I can't help but giggle in response.

After a few more cycles of thread, I feel truly empowered, like I'll finally be able to make sense of my questions. I lay the wax figure on a charged cotton handkerchief and take one last, long look at the body—sort of a greenish color now, a blending of clarity and mystery, now bridled by my mindfulness. I sprinkle the cut-up letters over it.

"So he won't get cold?" Amber asks.

"So the pieces will unite in my dreams," I correct. "When you have a better handle on things, the pieces tend to come together more completely."

"Uh, yeah, that's what I always say."

I smile at Amber's sarcasm and carefully roll the effigy up in the handkerchief. I place it under my pillow, confident that I will have insightful dreams tonight.

twenty-nine

I'm walking down a long, narrow corridor in the basement of the O'Brian building. It's dark except for the few yellowy light bulbs lined up overhead and quiet save for some dripping pipes along the ceiling—the sound of water hitting against the cement floor.

I fold my arms to soften the chill and make my way toward the end of the hallway, the floor littered with paint cans and other custodial supplies. There are doors lining the walls. I press my ear against one of them, but don't hear anything. I try the knob. Locked.

There's a sound coming from the door at the end. A rhythmic, slapping sound, followed by the thumping of feet against the pavement. Like someone's jumping rope.

"Hello?" I call, my voice echoing off the concrete walls.

But no one answers.

"Maura? Is that you?"

I take a few more steps, doing my best to make out any movement at the end of the hallway. But it's just so dim, the light bulbs overhead too sparse and dull to allow much more than shadows. I can see a shadow against the wall, just to the right of the door at the end of the hallway—a looplike shadow that rotates around and around.

I continue to walk toward the movement, toward the sound, and then I hear a voice—Maura's voice—singing:

> *Miss Mary Mack, Mack, Mack, all dressed in black, black, black. She has a knife, knife, knife, stuck in her back, back, back. She cannot breathe, breathe, breathe. She cannot cry, cry, cry. That's why she begs, begs, begs. She begs to die, die, die.*

A chill runs down the back of my neck. My heart starts pumping hard in my chest. I take another step and then stop. The shadow of her figure, jumping rope, is just a few yards away now. "Maura?"

She hears me. I've startled her, I think. The singing stops. The shadow pauses mid-rope-rotation, and the jump rope falls to the ground.

"It's Stacey," I say.

Her shadow squats down on the ground, as though to hide. And then I see the shadow of arm movement; she's drawing something on the ground—the letter M in dark red crayon.

"Maura?" I ask. "Your name? Is that what the M stands for?"

But instead of answering, she runs away—her shadow scampers along the wall, out of sight. Leaving me alone.

I move to the right to follow her, but stop, noticing the jump rope on the ground—not just the shadow but the real thing. I pick it up and sniff it. It smells like strawberry candy and buttered popcorn. Like her. The way I remember her.

"Maura?" I call.

I can hear her—the faint sound of her whimpering. It's coming from behind the door. I place my ear up against the door crack and can hear her clearly; she's crying, muttering my name between sobs, begging me to get her out.

I try the knob, but it's locked. I pull at it, kick it, place a foot up on the wall for better leverage, and yank the knob with all my might. But it's no use; the door won't budge.

"Maura—" I shout. "Can you help me? Can you open the door and let me in?" I jam my fingers into the door crack and do my best to pry it open that way. But I can't seem to wedge my fingers in deep enough. They keep slipping out, a couple all bloody from splinters.

Maura's crying louder now, almost screaming—a scared, horrible, and hopeless cry. I place my hands over my ears, and I hear myself cry out, too.

"Stacey—" she calls out between sobs.

"I'm here!" I yell into the door crack. "I'm not going to leave you."

I hear her body slide down against the door. Her crying is at knee-level now. I squat down to be closer to her. "Can you hear me?" I ask.

But the crying stops altogether.

"Maura?" I stand back up and pound on the door. "Are you still there? Are you okay?"

"I'm still here, Stacey," answers a male voice, one I don't readily recognize.

"Where's Maura?" I cry.

"Welcome back," he says.

"Where is she?" I kick and beat at the door with every ounce of energy left in me.

"Looking forward to our meeting?" he asks. "I've been waiting a long time."

"Who are you?" I take a step away from the door, awaiting some response, but there isn't any. After several seconds, I begin assessing the door—the hinges, the crack at the bottom, the knob. That's when I notice the keyhole. I run my fingers over the top of the door frame and find it— a rusty key with green paint splotches. I stick it into the lock and try the knob. This time it turns.

I take a step inside. It's even darker in here, the smell a mix of must and dampness. I move my hands to feel around the walls for a switch, but can't find one. Something sharp on the wall pricks an already bleeding finger. I stick my finger in my mouth and open the door up wider to let in some light from the hallway.

It appears as though this is a shed of some sort. There are tools hanging on the wall, a workbench to my right, and metal shelving to the left. I take a step closer, focusing on the pieces of folded paper lined up on the metal shelves—dozens upon dozens of origami pieces—birds of all types, cats, rabbits, frogs, snakes . . .

"Maura," I call. "Are you in here?" I move farther inside and the door shuts, a heavy slam. I feel my breath quicken, my heart pump inside my chest. It's completely dark now.

There's a shifting sound in the corner.

"Maura?" I whisper.

I can hear her coughing, getting sick. Like she might be choking on something.

I feel sick as well; my stomach is gurgling, clenching up like a fist. Arms outstretched, I move toward the corner where I think she might be hiding. But there's something blocking me from getting to her. I can't get past it—can't go around or climb over it. A heavy machine of some sort. My hands and neck are sweating. My mouth is dry, a thick, pasty film coating over my tongue.

There's a ringing sound from somewhere behind me. A phone, on the workbench, I think. It's Jacob. He has some information for me, something he has to tell me. I just know it.

I hold my stomach and turn around to find the phone. But instead I find tools. My jittery hands paw over them—a hammer, a wrench, some rusty nails, a fire extinguisher. Stuff I could use to get out of here—to break the door down.

Maura is still getting sick in the corner. The only way for me to help her is to find the phone, to find out what Jacob has to tell me. But the queasiness in my stomach is holding me in place.

"Stacey," a voice yells out. "Will you please just pick up the phone? It's closest to you!"

It's Amber's voice.

"Stacey?"

I wake up with a gasp—and sit up in bed. The phone is ringing from my night table.

Amber sits up in bed as well. "Do you want me to get it?" she asks.

I shake my head and pick up the phone, my heart still thrashing around in my chest, my face still sweating. "Hello? Jacob?"

"No, Stacey. It's Mom. Who's Jacob?"

"Hi, Mom," I say, noting the sour, sticky taste in my mouth. If Amber hadn't woken me up, I'd probably be covered in yack right about now. I give Amber the okay sign and she responds by flopping back in bed. She rolls over and draws the covers up over her head.

I look at the clock. It's after midnight. "Are you okay?" I ask my mother.

"I just couldn't sleep," she says. "I'm sorry it's so late. I've just been worried about you. Who's Jacob?"

"Just some guy," I say. "A friend. Wait—why are you worried?"

"Because of what you said—about having nightmares."

I take a deep breath and let it out slowly. I really don't want to go through this again with her. Not now. Right now I want to call Jacob. The dream just felt so real. Like he really has something to tell me, something I need to know.

"I think maybe you should try to preoccupy yourself with some hobby," she says.

"*What?*"

"A hobby," she repeats, her voice wavering over the word.

"Are you *serious?*"

"Get involved in a club at school, maybe—something artistic." She continues after a pause, "Or try a sport. Maybe socializing with kids with different interests might help relax you a bit. I've been doing a lot of online research about nightmares and it seems people who experience them do so because they have no other outlets for stress."

A hobby? Something artistic? It's almost twelve-freaking-thirty in the morning. Is she out of her mind?

"Can we talk about this later?" I ask.

"Sure, honey. I just wanted to call and tell you that. And to tell you that I'm thinking about you. And I love you."

"I know you do, Mom."

"Okay, honey."

There's silence between us for several seconds. It's almost like she has something else to tell me, some other agenda. But we just remain quiet, listening to each other breathe. Part of me wants to tell her that I love her back, but I'm too annoyed. And I know that's probably selfish, that she obviously really does care about me to call at this late hour, to feel so plagued about it. But there's another part inside me that feels bitter, resentful that she doesn't take me more seriously. Especially after everything I've been through.

We hang up shortly after. The slip of paper Jacob gave me with his phone number scribbled across it is sitting on my nightstand. I dial his number.

"Stacey?" he answers.

"Yeah," I whisper. "How did you know?"

"I tried calling but your line was busy. I figured you'd call."

"We need to talk," I say.

"Yeah," he agrees. "We do. Can you meet me tonight?"

My heart starts pumping even harder. Because I'm scared. Because he's so urgent. Because it's him and I don't know what to expect. I glance over at Amber and Drea, asleep in their bunks. "Okay," I say. "Where?"

We arrange to meet in the laundry room by the underclasswoman dorms. I stuff a wad of clothes into a pillowcase to make it look legit, cram my feet into a pair of sneakers, and grab my coat and flashlight. I make my way quietly through the lobby and out the front door, noticing right away that the front door isn't locked. But I don't have time to dwell on it, because just in front of me, looped around the branch of the cypress tree in front of our dorm, is a rope of some sort. The overhead spotlights shine right over it, swinging in the breeze.

I descend the steps and approach it slowly. I know it's for me and I know what it is. And I'm right. It's a jump rope—just like the one in my dream. Except this one's tied into a noose.

thirty

The jump-rope-turned-noose hangs from a branch just overhead, the two plastic handles dangling down in front of my eyes. I take a couple steps away from it and cover my mouth, shaking my head like this isn't real, like it can't be true. A whistlelike sound sputters from my mouth. My name is written in thick black marker down each of the handles, so there's no doubting that it's for me—that someone wants to kill me.

"Stacey?" says a voice from behind me. A male voice, one I don't recognize right away.

I feel my shoulders stiffen, my jaw lock.

"It's me," he says.

I turn to look. It's Jacob, partially concealed in shadows.

"Are you okay?" he asks, taking a step forward. He looks up at the noose and then makes his way toward it. "What's that?" he asks.

"What are you doing here?" I tighten my grip on the laundry bag, feeling the ample weight at the bottom. If I need to I can use it to fight.

He pulls the rope from the branch and runs his thumbs over the handles, maybe trying to sense something from my name.

"I *said*, what are you doing here?"

"What do you mean?" he asks. "We were supposed to meet."

"In the laundry room," I say. "On the other side of campus."

"I know," he says. "I just didn't think you should be walking around by yourself at night."

"How thoughtful," I say, looking at the noose in his hands, wondering if he's the one who left it for me.

"As soon as I hung up the phone with you, I sprinted over here so I wouldn't miss you," he says, now trying to sense something from the rope fibers. "Do you have any idea who could have put this here?"

"Maybe you could tell me," I say, taking note that he's fully dressed, that his hair looks slightly wet, as though from gel—like maybe he wasn't in bed at all.

"Hmm—" he says, pausing at the knotted part, ignoring my remark.

"What?" I ask.

"Do you mind if I take this? I might be able to use it. I might be able to find out who put it here."

"I don't think so," I say, grabbing the noose from him. I feel over the handles as well, the tips of my fingers still tingling from getting pricked and splintered in my dream. I check them over for cuts, but there aren't any. And I can't seem to sense anything but my own fear.

"We should talk," he says. "But not here. Do you still want to go to the laundry room?"

I shake my head. All I really want to do is go back inside, beneath the haven of my covers, and start this night all over again. I tighten my grip on the rope, hoping to squeeze any sign, any clue, any *anything* out. But it's like my hand is numb, unfeeling.

"How about in the boiler room of your dorm?" he asks. "I know the way in."

As though I could forget. "I don't think so," I say.

"Then where?" he asks.

For just a second I think about telling him to leave, that we have nothing to say to one another. But, all considered, I know I should hear him out. My dreams and the letter are telling me that I have less than a week to figure this out. Less than a week—which could be just a couple days away. Or closer. For all I know, it could be tomorrow. Or tonight.

I look over at the benches on the lawn, the heavy spotlights shining over them. "There," I say. Before Jacob can answer, I clasp my hand over the crystal cluster rock in my pocket and start walking over to the spot.

"You know, we could get caught here. It's way after curfew."

"I don't really care," I say. "I don't even know why we had to meet. Why couldn't we have just talked on the phone?"

"I can sense more about you when we're together," he replies.

"And what are you sensing now?" I ask.

"That you're in serious danger."

I stop to look at him. "Is that why you were trying to call me tonight?"

"I could ask you the same thing," he says. "Why did *you* call *me*?"

I take a seat on the bench. "Because I thought we needed to talk."

Jacob sits down next to me. He's nodding, his stare so penetrating, like he can see right inside me, into that faraway corner of myself, the place that I never reveal—not even to Chad. Chad. I look away and try to zap him into my mind—to remind myself that he's the one I love, the one I care about. And yet our relationship has been such a complete and utter mess, after months and months of near perfection.

"I had another nightmare about you tonight," Jacob says, zapping me back in place.

I venture a look at his face, noticing for the first time the mole under his bottom lip. "About what?"

"About you getting sick."

"Sick how?"

"Like sick to your stomach. Like hangover-sick—with vomiting."

"You probably just dreamed that because puking has become a sort of spectator sport for me lately. I think people have dubbed me the exorcist chick."

He settles back into the bench and looks away, like there's something else on his mind, something he's not telling me.

"What?" I ask.

"Nothing," he says.

"Not nothing."

"It's just I think there's more to it, that's all."

"Like what? What else did you dream about?"

"Hands," he says, looking back at me.

"Hands?"

He nods. "Encircling your neck."

"What do you mean?"

"I mean I think someone is going to try and strangle you."

"Then what's with the noose?"

Jacob shakes his head. "It's like someone's trying to scare you. It's, like, either you pursue them, or they'll come after you."

"Who?"

"I don't know. But I'm pretty sure it's someone you already know."

"How do you know that?"

"Because when it happens, when the two of you come face-to-face, it's like you aren't afraid of the person—at least not at first. It's like you're almost expecting him."

"Him? So it's a guy?"

He shakes his head. "I can't be sure. The hands look pretty strong, but I haven't been able to see much detail about them yet."

"What *do* you see?" I ask.

"I can see the hands constrict, and I can see you . . . choking."

I try to swallow the image, but it won't get past my throat. I let out a gasp and then cover my mouth to try and hold it all in.

"Are you all right?" Jacob asks. He touches my shoulder. "Maybe I shouldn't have told you."

"No. It's okay. I'll be okay." I shake my head, trying to get the image of it—of someone's hands encircling my neck, putting me to death—out of my head. But instead the image presses against my chest. I do my best to look up at the full moon and breathe its energy in, but instead I feel like the air is blocked, like I'm coming apart and there's nothing I can do about it.

Jacob's hand slips across my shoulders, until it wraps around me. "I know you'll be okay," he says quietly, firmly. "Because I'm going to help you."

A part of me wants to wipe his hand away, but I don't. Because there's a bigger part—a weaker part, maybe—that needs comfort right now. I keep my focus away from him so I don't reveal too much, even though I know I'm being so pathetically transparent. "I don't even know you," I say, wiping at my eyes. "It doesn't even make sense."

"What doesn't?"

"Why you started dreaming about me in the first place. You didn't even know me. When I was having nightmares about Drea and Maura, it was different. I knew them. They were important people in my life."

Jacob nestles me in closer, so close I can feel his chest now, moving in and out with each breath. And I can smell him. He smells like lemongrass incense—a smell I want to breathe right into my skin. I close my eyes, trying my hardest to get hold of my emotions, to breathe the tension out. We sit there for several seconds without saying a word.

"I'm sorry," I say, regaining a bit of strength. I sit back up and look into his face, so close to mine, his squarish chin just inches from my forehead.

"It's okay," he says. He lays a hand over my coat pocket and feels the crystal inside, sensing somehow that I'd be carrying it. "We're connected in some way. Why else would I be dreaming about your future? How else would I know you've been having nightmares about Maura, and about Veronica Leeman? Haven't you considered that?"

I suppose I have. I suppose it's the connection he's talking about that has me all jangled up whenever I'm around him. I tug my coat away from his hand and focus down into my lap, doing my best to suppress the blush I feel crawling across my cheeks. I hate myself for feeling this way—now, of all times, when my life is at stake, when I'm having serious boyfriend issues. I take a deep breath to stifle the confusion and frustration I feel storming up inside my chest, in my mouth, and behind my eyes.

"How do you know what I dream about?" I ask.

"I just know," he says. "I can't explain it. I just feel things. I see things—sometimes while I'm sleeping, sometimes not."

I nod and look away, too emotionally spent to ask him more about it. And besides, I know exactly what he's talking about—how he and I are so completely alike in this way.

"Say something," he says.

"Like what?" I swallow, looking back at him. At his eyes.

"Like you believe me, like you believe I can help you."

"I can't be sure of anything right now," I say.

"What can I say or do to make you sure?" he asks.

I think about it a moment, and the question becomes obvious. "How am I supposed to know you're really from Colorado, that you really came all the way here to try and help me?"

Without hesitation, Jacob pulls a wallet from his pocket and shows me a couple forms of picture ID—a driver's license from Vail, Colorado, along with a school ID card with his name and address.

"Okay, so if you really came all this way, just for me, then why did it take over two months to come out and contact me . . . I mean, if I was in so much danger . . ."

"Because I was afraid," he answers.

"*Afraid? Afraid of what?*"

"Of *this*. Of you not believing me. I wanted to watch for a while." He pauses. "And I wanted to dream about you more."

"You were watching me?" I ask, remembering the words written on the cassette tape left in our room.

"Look," he says, "I know you don't trust me. And with all the freaks around this campus, I'm not even sure I can give you a reason why you should, but I have no reason to lie. With or without my help, someone is going to try and hurt you. And if we don't do anything about it, I think they might succeed."

I glance down at the noose, still gripped in my hand. "I don't trust anyone."

"Not even Chad?" he asks.

"Leave him out of this."

"I can't," he says, biting his lip, staring down at my own.

"Why?"

"Because I can't." He turns away, leaving me hungry for more.

I'm tempted to ask him again, but I don't. Because maybe I'm just not ready to know . . . and maybe I already know.

"I should go," I say.

"No," he says, touching my arm. "I'm sorry. I don't know what's wrong with me."

I don't know what's wrong with me either. We sit in silence, both of us knowing we should say our goodnights but neither of us making a move. After several awkward moments, Jacob sits up and leans into me, his face so close I can smell his skin, that lemongrass scent. I do my best to look away—I blink. I look up at the moon. I even try reminding myself of the horrific reality of the noose still clutched in my hand. But nothing works. Jacob's pale-blue eyes stare right into me, almost paralyzing me in place. He leans in a little closer, and I feel my lips part.

"Stacey?" says a voice.

It's Chad.

My heart clenches. I press my eyes closed in disbelief, at how unbelievably stupid I am, and then turn around to face him.

Chad glances back and forth between me and Jacob.

"Chad," I say, standing up. "It's not—" But I can't even finish the thought. Chad looks so completely confused—his face scrunched up like he doesn't understand. He looks away, as if the picture of Jacob and me, here, like this, hurts too much—as if *I've* hurt him too much this time.

"I can explain," I tell him, thinking how unbelievably trite that sounds.

Jacob gets up and stands beside me. "It's not what you're thinking," he says. "It's been a bad night."

"Apparently, just for some people." Chad takes one last look at me before turning and walking away, making me feel even worse.

"I'm sorry," Jacob says. "Do you want me to go talk to him?"

"No," I say. "I will."

I just hope Chad is willing to listen.

thirty-one

I try my best to catch up to Chad—I circle the dorm, run down the path that leads toward the center of campus, and even scour the parking lot area. But he's nowhere in sight.

I end up going back inside the dorm, where I find Drea and Amber, wide awake and waiting for me.

"Where have you *been?*" Amber asks.

"It's a long story," I say, moving toward the phone receiver. I pick it up, dial Chad's number, but get voicemail right away. "Chad, it's me. Please call me back. I need to talk to you. Please . . ." I click the phone off, shaking my head that I didn't say more, that I really don't know what to say.

"Chad's on his way *here*," Drea says.

"What are you talking about?"

"I called him. When I woke up and saw you weren't here, or anywhere around here for that matter, I thought you might have sneaked out with him somewhere. So I called him to be sure."

"I wasn't meeting Chad," I say.

"I know," Drea says. "That's why he freaked. You can't just take off in the middle of the night, Stacey. Not with everything that's going on."

"So uncool," Amber says, untwisting her legs from the lotus position.

"Which is why Chad's coming over," Drea says. "We were all really worried about you."

"Well, he's not coming now," I say, flopping down on my bed.

"Why? What do you mean?"

I tell her and Amber what happened—how I had another nightmare, which prompted me to meet Jacob; how I found the noose; and how Chad spotted me and Jacob sitting on the bench together and got all jealous about it.

Amber jumps up and nabs the noose from me. She sticks a leg into the loop part and pulls it up like some sort of string bikini. "Maybe you and witch-boy were planning something kinky."

"It's a freaking noose, Amber," I shout.

"I've heard of weirder fetishes," she says.

"So what *did* Chad see exactly?" Drea asks.

"He just saw us talking," I say.

"Oh, please," Amber says. "I can tell when you're lying, Stacey—your lips get all puckery. It totally had to be more than just that! Dish, please."

"What?" I say, looking away. "Fine—he may have thought we were gonna kiss."

"You *kissed* witch-boy?" Amber says. "Details, please."

"I didn't kiss anyone," I say. "Can we please get back to my life being at stake here?"

"Was it magically delicious?" Amber persists.

I slump back on my bed and bury my face in a pillow. If it weren't a Saturday I think I just might resort to taking a trip to the school shrink today. *That's* how desperate I feel.

"So," Amber begins in an effort to redeem herself, "Jacob said he had a nightmare about you being throttled to death—hands clamping around your neck, thumbs digging into your throat, blocking off all the air, sending you to the land of complete and utter oblivion."

"Thanks for the thorough recap," I say.

"So, obviously that's why someone left you a noose," she says. "For choking."

I look up at her. She's got the loop part of the noose crowning her head now, the handles dangling over her shoulders like braids. "It isn't a toy," I say.

"Actually," she says, "it is."

Drea gives Amber the evil-eye blink and then focuses back on me. "Why a jump rope?" she asks.

"I don't know," I say, sitting back up, "but in my night-mare, Maura was jumping rope."

"So it's a clue," Drea says. "About what's going to hap-pen."

"Either that," Amber says, "or someone can see into your dreams and therefore knows Maura's jumping rope in them. A witch-boy, perhaps." She arches her eyebrows up and down.

"Don't you think that's a little obvious?" I ask. "Why would someone tell me he can see into my dreams and then leave me a key prop from one of them? It's a dead giveaway."

"Nice choice of words," Amber says.

"I saw the origami snake in my nightmare," I say.

"Did it say anything?" Drea asks.

"When was the last time a paper snake spoke to you?" Amber asks.

"No," Drea says, rolling her eyes. "I mean, did she unfold it? Was there a message inside?"

I shake my head. "I was too busy looking for Maura. But there was lots of origami—like a whole collection."

"So what you're telling me," Amber begins, "is that this psycho stalker folds pretty squares of colored paper in his spare time?"

"I don't know."

"That's so random."

"But it does tell us something," Drea says. "At least now we can eliminate people as suspects. I mean, how many origami artists do we know?"

"What if he's a closet origami artist?" Amber asks. She folds her history quiz up into a paper airplane and shoots it at Drea's head.

"I saw the letter *M*, too," I say. "Maura drew it on the ground in red crayon. She used to do that from time to time—color on the pavement with crayons and then wait for the wax to melt in the sun, so it would get all blurry."

"It's like she's trying to tell you something," Drea says.

"But what?" I ask.

"I think we should call campus police," Drea says.

"Are you kidding?" I gasp. "Do you have any idea how much they hate me? Do you know how many times I've called them this year? Between stupid prank notes tacked up on our door, to all those bogus phone calls, to the time someone left that cardboard knife on my desk during English?"

"Let's not forget the ketchup-blood mural someone so lovingly painted in your honor," Amber says.

"Or those funeral-supply catalogs you started getting in the mail," Drea says.

"Exactly," I say. "A jump-rope-turned-noose is just another thing campus police can add to their list about me. A list that's probably entitled 'the top hundred-and-two reasons why Stacey Brown should have transferred schools last year.'" I click the phone back on and try Chad's number again, but he's still not answering.

"He must be really upset," Drea says.

"I know," I say.

"Nothing that a little schnookie won't cure," Amber says, puckering up.

"I don't know," Drea says. "It really hurts when someone you care about betrays you like that."

"I didn't betray him."

Drea reaches into the fridge for a bar of chocolate. She takes a bite and looks away. I know she must be thinking otherwise. And maybe she's right. I mean, who am I really kidding here? I just don't know what's wrong with me. First I betray my best friend, and now I'm betraying my boyfriend. And all the while what I should really be focusing on is the fact that my life is at stake and that I have less than a week before I could wind up dead.

thirty-two

Completely riddled with guilt, I try calling Chad a bunch more times but he never picks up. So I end up waiting it out until seven, when all us prisoners are allowed to walk freely about campus and actually visit other dorms. But when I get to Chad's, he isn't there. I check the hockey rink, the gym, the pool, the cafeteria, and every last corner of the library. No luck.

My last resort—the Hangman. I peel the door open, a sudden gust of mochaccino fumes hitting me in the face, and look around at the individual tables. The place is pretty packed—kids opting for café fare over the cafeteria's scrambled egg surprise—but Chad is nowhere in sight.

I decide to try and swallow a bit of my guilt with a cheese danish. I order myself one, along with a cup of Colombian brew, and take a seat in the corner of the stage section. This might actually be the perfect spot for me this morning—a place where I can be by myself and think, where I don't have to worry about bumping into anyone important.

That's when I notice Trish and Emma coming out of the bathroom. They take a seat with Cory, sitting in the back of the audience section, typing away on a laptop. I can't believe I didn't notice him before. I scoot my chair back against the stage curtain, hoping they don't see me. But they do. First Trish, who graciously waves in my direction, and then the others. They point, talk amongst themselves, and then start laughing, like this is middle school.

Cory closes up his laptop and makes his way over to my table. He takes a seat across from me. "So, come here often?" He's giggling at his lame little line, the gap between his two front teeth stuffed up with what looks like lemon jelly.

"Hysterical," I say.

"Thanks." He glances back at Trish and Emma, staring at us over mugs of frothy java drinks.

"What do you want?" I ask.

"What?" he says. "I can't just come over here and wish you a pleasant day?"

I ignore him by taking a bite of pastry and reading the little jingle printed on the side of my coffee cup—something about morning perks in Central Park.

"How long do you think you'll be able to keep that down?"

"What are you talking about?"

"You know? Before you purge the splurge? Toss the caloric cookies? Don't think I haven't heard about your little vomit attacks. You know they have eating disorder clinics for stuff like that."

"Go away," I say.

"Actually," he leans in closer, "Veronica Leeman doesn't want me to. She tells me I should stick pretty close to you, keep an eye on you."

"Is this from your so-called séance?"

"I prefer to call it a communion with souls. Care to attend our communion tomorrow night? Veronica's been asking for you."

"Don't you have some tables to wipe?" I ask.

"Why?" He gets up from the table, the jam between his two front teeth bulging out even further now, like a giant booger. "I don't work here."

"What do you mean? You worked here a couple days ago."

"Nope." He smiles. "I wouldn't work in a place like this. Sort of creepy, don't you think? Haunted with old souls . . . You know, legend has it some girl hung herself in here."

"Haven't we been through this before?"

"Really, Stacey," he says, "you must have me confused with someone else."

He gets up and leaves, and I feel even more confused and irritated than ever. I look over at his table as he makes his way back there, and I almost can't believe what I'm seeing—Donna Tillings is sitting with them.

I feel my mouth drop open. I can just imagine how they must be using her, how they must be so completely salivating over her past connection with Veronica Leeman.

I crumple the remainder of my pastry up into a napkin, completely devoid of appetite, and get up to leave. But instead of succeeding with my getaway I'm shocked back into place. The door swings open and PJ shimmies in. He makes his way over to Cory and his clones.

It appears as though he's joining them all for breakfast, which completely surprises me, seeing that he doesn't even hang out with them. Seeing that yesterday, in the library, Cory and that Tobias guy came so close to showing PJ first hand where he could shoot his water pistol.

PJ nabs a doughnut from Emma's plate as soon as she looks away and stuffs the entire thing in his mouth. And then, mouth full, he attempts to talk to Donna, even though he and Donna have absolutely nothing in common, even though last year they seemed so repelled by one another that they couldn't even be in the same room together, let alone eat breakfast at the same table.

I watch PJ swallow hard and turn to Cory. They start gabbing away like old best friends. Like yesterday's confrontation in the library was just as staged as this stupid café.

I feel the tiny hairs at the back of my neck popping up like some cartoonish rendition of anger. Cory directs PJ's attention toward me. PJ waves, but I don't wave back. Instead I bolt down the stage steps, nearly colliding with Tobias on the way. He passes in front of me dressed in café garb—a long red apron over a T-shirt with a pair of theatrical masks silk-screened to the front—and holding a tray of sticky bun samples.

"What's the rush?" he says, checking the tray for spillage. He takes a wide stance in the aisle, blocking my path to the exit door.

"Unless you want to be wearing those sticky buns," I say, "you better get out of my way."

"Jeez, Stacey, you don't look too good. Rough night last night? Did you not get enough sleep?"

My jaw locks. It's all I can do to hold myself back from shoving the tray of sticky buns right into that stupid, self-satisfied smirk on his face, at the nervous twitch of his eye. At least now I know how Cory got in here that night, when he told campus police he was closing up shop. I push my way past Tobias and head for the exit door, but PJ intercepts me.

"Wait!" PJ says.

"I don't have time."

He pulls me to the side and lowers his voice. "This isn't what it looks like."

"And what *does* it look like?" I whisper back.

"It looks like I'm getting all jammy with Computer Cory and the Caged-Bird Clonesters."

"*What?*"

He grazes his palm over the tips of his plum-purple hair spikes. "You know those ghost groupies aren't my style."

"It doesn't look that way to me."

"Precisely, my dear Wordsworth," he says, with a wink. "Precisely."

"You're not making any sense."

"Trust me," he says, "I'd make a lot more sense if you were to treat me to a couple cinnamon scones and indulge me in a bit of morning chatter."

"Forget it," I say, going for the door.

"Forget me not," he says, grabbing my arm and holding me in place. "We need to dish, little girl. And *tout de suite*. I've got the scoop on you, the old Chadster, and some unidentified mystery man. I think you have some explaining to do."

Obviously he's talked to Chad, which is probably the only reason I do end up indulging him in conversation instead of rushing back to the dorm to nurse the throbbing in my head. *That* and the fact that I want to know what he's up to with Cory and the others.

PJ apologizes to them about having to leave so abruptly, and we take off right after, despite PJ's squawks about not eating breakfast.

"So what's going on?" I ask, as soon as we get outside. "Since when do you hang out with Cory and Donna and them?"

"First answer my question, sweet pea," he says. "What's this I hear about you and some mystery boy sexing it up under the stars? I want the lowdown. Better yet, I want the Polaroids."

We take a seat on one of the benches in the quad area. "Is that what Chad said happened?"

"It's what I heard, O feisty one," PJ says.

"Well, you heard wrong."

PJ shrugs. "According to you."

"So, he's mad?"

"As a hornet. Wouldn't you be, my little bumblebee? All sting-y?" He buzzes for effect, making me feel like a complete and utter idiot for even attempting to get the details from him.

"So now answer my question," I say. "What's with you and your new friends?"

"I'm only hanging out with them for you, love bug," he says.

"What do you mean?"

He bustles up the front of his coat and pulls a pair of fingerless gloves from his pocket. "Just call me double-o-seven."

"Why?"

"Because I'm a spy." He squints his eyes for drama. "You know, a double agent."

"A little reality, please."

"You're no fun." He slips the gloves on and blows at his fingers for warmth. "Can I tell you how hungry I am? No wonder I'm so cold."

"Can you please tell me what you're talking about?"

"Food? You know? My need for some."

"PJ . . ." I sigh.

"Fine," he says, rolling his eyes. "Cory stopped by my room last night and we had this long and dishy powwow, and, well, he wants me to help out at the séance."

"Are you kidding me? Why would he ever ask you to join the séance?"

"Isn't it obvious?" PJ asks. "I'm oozing with spiritual energy."

"Seriously," I say.

"Okay, seriously, it's because me and Veronica had a past. He's hoping that past will help fuel the ol' spiritual fire— you know, ignite the cosmic forces of the seventh sign."

"You have no idea what you're even talking about."

"Oh contraire," he says. "I know all about cosmetological forces."

"That's *cosmological* forces," I say, rolling my eyes. "And that has nothing to do with channeling spirits. Bottom line—you and Veronica had no past; you hated each other. So why would she want to talk to you in the afterlife?"

"She only hated me because she wasn't able to get over me. Poor thing—I wouldn't give the damsel the time of day." He breathes on his fist and then rubs it across his chest, bravado-style.

"You're so full of crap," I say.

"Details, schmetails," PJ says. "Bottom line, as you so slinkily put it, the ghost groupies need my mind; they need my impassioned energy, my unadulterated aura."

"And what do you get out of it?"

"Whatever do you mean, my little jar of jelly?"

"You must be getting something. You wouldn't just do this for nothing."

"I'm doing it for you."

"Tell me!" I demand.

"I'm insulted."

"And I'm leaving." I get up from the bench.

"So, does this mean you're *not* going to treat me to breakfast?"

I feel my teeth clench.

"Okay," he says. "Would it make you feel better if I told you they may have thrown in a couple homework assignments to sweeten the deal?"

"Homework assignments?"

"And maybe a couple term papers. But that's absolutely it. I think you should be grateful."

"*Grateful?*"

"Yeah, at first I thought it was a total dish of dung, but then I got to thinking and figured, hey, this might be my little way of helping out my good friend Stacey. You know? Like, get you some valuable scoop on what's going jiggy with all of them. They've got Donna in on it too."

"Why would Donna ever agree to help them?"

"Oh, please," PJ says. "Donna's a total dweeboid this year. And what do dweeboids look for, I ask you?"

"You tell me."

He sighs like it's obvious. "Fellow dweeboids to fill their time."

"That's obviously why you're doing it."

"*Touché, mademoiselle,*" he says. "Aren't you Miss Sharpie with that tongue of yours?"

"I have to go," I say.

"Not so fast, my little jack rabbit. The groupies have asked me if I can try and strong-arm your little behind into joining us in the next communion with souls. How's that for fancy titles?"

"I think I have a better title for you," I say.

"And what's that?"

"Idiot."

I leave him there on the bench, buzzing away, as I make my way across the lawn. Between him and the whole fiasco at the Hangman, I think I've wasted enough time for one day. I need to get back to the room and work the gigantic jigsaw pieces of my life back into place—before it's too late.

thirty-three

When I get back to the room, Drea has already left—but re-placing her, sitting on my bed, is the last person I want to see right now.

My mother.

She looks up at me, a broad and beaming smile stretched across her face, like she couldn't be happier to see me.

"Hi, honey," she says.

It looks like Amber has been keeping her thoroughly entertained. She's got her shoebox full of memorabilia dumped out on the bed, showing my mother all her sentimental trinkets.

My mother gets up and wraps her arms around me. "It's so good to see you."

"What are you doing here?" I ask, hugging her back. I look over my mother's shoulder at Amber, who shakes her head like she doesn't know either.

"I thought we could use a chat," she says, breaking the embrace.

I stand there nodding, wanting to say something considerate, since she's just driven three whole hours to see me, but blanking on all the considerate words in my immediate vocabulary. "You could have called," I say, cringing at the sound of my own bitchiness. It's just that with everything that's going on and my mother's obvious desire to live in La La Land and see that I start some meaningless hobby like macramé or needlepoint, it's not a good time.

"I was going to call you after we hung up last night," my mother says, "but it was so late, and I couldn't go back to sleep, so I just started driving. I'm staying at a hotel downtown."

"You're *staying*?"

"Just for the day. I wasn't so sure I'd be up for the drive back tonight."

I nod, looking to Amber for a diversion. She's puckering up to a disco-garbed Ken doll, complete with gold lamé pants and dangling medallion. She kisses him so hard his head pops off and rolls to the floor.

"Aren't you glad to see me?" my mother asks.

"Of course I am." I hug her again. She smells like home, like lily-of-the-valley perfume mixed in grape-scented hair spray. I kick Ken's head toward Amber's feet, but she's so into her snuggle down memory lane with him she doesn't even notice his recent decapitation.

"So, shall we go to brunch?" my mother asks. She turns to Amber. "Amber, will you join us? And Drea, too. Is she around?"

Amber shakes her head. "Drea took off with Chad."

"Where?" I ask.

Amber shrugs. "He came by. Probably to see you. But you'd already left."

So freaking fabulous. I sink down into my bed and burrow my face into my hands. All I want to do right now is talk to Chad, to tell him I'm sorry, to try my hardest to fix everything, to grab my pillow and scream into it at the top of my lungs in frustration.

"Stacey, are you okay?" my mother asks, like it isn't already obvious.

I lift my head from my hands and fake a smile.

"Don't mind her," Amber says, "Stacey's just been a little constipated lately."

My mother clears her throat in response, and I can't help but giggle.

"So," my mother turns to Amber, "will you join us for breakfast?"

"I don't think so," Amber says. "I sort of already have something started here." She gazes down at her nostalgia trinkets—a Silly Putty egg, a box of Sweethearts, a couple friendship bracelets, and a wide array of Ken clothes, from swim shorts to hiking boots. She presses a headless Ken into her bosom.

"I'm not gonna ask," I say.

"That's probably best," Amber says, retrieving Ken's head from the floor.

I grab a handful of pine needles from the vase, hoping the smell of pine mixed with the healing quality of the needles will help dispel the negativity I feel bubbling up in my stomach.

It's pretty quiet between my mother and me as we drive into town. I roll the pine needles between the tips of my fingers and remind myself that my mother's surprise visit is a loving gesture. She's obviously really concerned about me, obviously thinks that whisking me away from campus is exactly what I need right now. And maybe she's right. Except, with each street that passes, I feel this giant, burning pit form just below my ribs—a pit that seems to deepen with each breath, reminding me that I don't have time to waste.

"Is everything okay?" my mother asks.

It's amazing how different she looks, even after just a couple months. Her hair is shorter and darker, like she just had it done, the sides a bit less fluffy than usual, curled behind her ears in a sort of tucked bob. She smiles at me, her lips paler than normal, a few shades off from the burgundy color I'm used to her wearing.

I nod as best I can, but I know I'm not fooling her. There's a different air about her today—more aware than usual, less detached.

We arrive at the Egg and I, a fifties-style diner complete with jukebox, black and white checkerboard floor, and old Elvis records nailed to the wall. We take a seat in the corner booth by the windows.

"What looks yummy?" she asks, peeling open her vinyl menu.

I choose the peanut butter pancakes since it's the first thing on the menu I see—a giant, colorful picture, complete with syrup and melting butter, taking up a large portion of the right side of the menu.

"Sounds good," she says. "I think I'll have the same."

For the next twenty minutes or so, we end up maintaining our usual pleasant yet meaningless chitchat. Not even the sugar in the pancakes or the caffeine in our bottomless cups of coffee have succeeded in moving either of us to say anything relevant. I just don't feel well. The pit in my gut feels like it's getting bigger with each chew, forcing me to feign a healthy appetite, i.e., to cut up my pancakes into tiny syrup-saturated pieces, to chase said pieces around the plate with my fork, and to pretend to chew them down like everything's normal. Like the possibility of my being murdered is so far from my thoughts right now.

My mother leans back against the vinyl seat and just stares at me, the mug of coffee pressed up against her bottom lip. "Not feeling well?" she asks.

I shake my head and set my fork down.

"I didn't think so."

"There's just been a lot of stuff going on," I say.

"I know," she says. "Which is why we *really* need to talk."

I pick my fork back up and start raking through the puddle of syrup on my plate.

"Are you listening to me?" she asks.

I nod, focusing on the prong impressions as I drag my fork through the golden goo. It's not that I don't think she means well. I do. It's just that I don't feel like getting into this with her again, especially since I know she doesn't take my nightmares seriously.

She grabs my wrist and forces me to look up at her. "I'm talking to you," she says.

I straighten up in the booth and wipe my mouth. "I know."

"So I expect you to listen."

"Okay."

She releases her grip on my wrist. "There's something I need to tell you about nightmares."

"Okay?" I say, a question in the reply.

"You need to pay attention to them," she says.

"I do?" I feel my teeth bite down on the inside of my cheek, completely baffled by what she's saying.

"I know you already know that," she says. "I just wanted you to hear it from me."

"Okay," I nod, trying to swallow down the mind-muddling effect of her words.

"I know you've had nightmares before," she continues. "Bad ones. And I also know they've warned you about the future."

"Where is all this coming from?" I ask. "I mean, why are you acknowledging it now?"

She doesn't answer, just focuses on her coffee cup, like it will answer for her.

"I want you to know that I knew about Maura," she says after a three-sip pause. "I knew you were having nightmares about her. I just didn't want you to know I did." My mother holds her napkin over her mouth, like that will change the meaning of her words, make them seem less harsh.

"What are you saying?"

"I'm saying that I wasn't completely honest with you back then, but it's only because I wanted the nightmares to stop. I thought that maybe if you focused on something else, they would."

"They didn't," I say.

"I know," she says, looking up from her coffee mug. "I'm sorry."

"Sorry?" My voice rises up at least three full octaves. "Do you know what that was like? Maura *died* because I didn't do anything about those nightmares. Because you didn't want to talk about them. Grandma was dead; I had no one else to turn to."

"I'm sorry," she repeats, her eyes filling up.

"Well, I'm sorry, too," I say. "Because that's just not good enough." I slide out from the booth.

"No, Stacey, wait," she says.

"Why?"

"Because I'm not finished yet."

"What else can you say? There's nothing that will make it better. Do you have any idea how alone I felt? The guilt I've had to live with? I loved Maura like a sister."

"I know," she manages, barely able to get the words out. "I know about guilt." She swallows hard and shakes her head, like she doesn't want to tell me. "It happened to me, too."

"What did?" I sit back down.

She grabs another napkin from the dispenser and holds it up to her face. "When I was seven, I had nightmares that my cousin Julia was going to die . . . and she did. An accident. She was fifteen years old and she drowned."

"Julia?"

"I might have mentioned her name to you once or twice."

I'm looking at my mother and shaking my head. It's like I have no idea who she really is.

"I saw the whole thing in my dream before it happened," she continues. "I even knew the day. She came to my house, asked me if I wanted to go to the lake with her. I can still picture it. She was wearing these bright pink sandals that had matching silk flowers on the straps. And she had a pink and green striped towel draped around her neck."

"Did you go?"

She shakes her head. "I was too scared."

My mother blots her eyes with the napkin and proceeds to tell me how she never told anyone about her nightmares—not even Gram—because they scared her too much. Because Gram used to tell her that sometimes what we dream about does indeed come true.

"At least in your case with Maura," my mother says, "someone was arrested and went to jail. He had to pay for his crime. In my situation, there was no one else to blame but me."

"Miles Parker didn't get nearly the punishment that he should have," I say. "He killed her—no matter how much they tried to call it an accident. They found rope and a hunting knife in his car, for god's sake."

"At least he's in prison now," my mother says, "where he belongs."

"Maybe he is," I say. "Or maybe he's plotting to do it again—kidnap another little girl."

"Stacey . . ." my mother squawks.

"I know," I say, taking a deep and calming breath.

For the next several seconds, my mother and I just sort of sit there in the booth, staring into our mugs, not really knowing what to say. A part of me wants to hug her and tell her that I understand, that I forgive her for not taking my nightmares more seriously. But I don't, because it doesn't make sense. Because it seems that after experiencing something so tragic, she should have wanted to help me, to listen to me all the more.

I press the coffee cup to my lips and fake a sip; I just don't know what else to do or say right now. There's a mixture of sadness and anger lingering inside my mouth. I want to tell her I'm sorry. I want to tell her that the tragedy of her cousin's death, of experiencing firsthand what can happen when you ignore your nightmares, makes it so much worse. It almost would have been better if she never told me all of this, if she just let me go on thinking that she didn't understand this part of me.

"What are you thinking?" she asks.

I shake my head since now it's me who doesn't understand.

"After the death," she continues, "I did everything in my power to stop from dreaming—I tried staying up all night, I'd force myself to wake up every hour. After a while it worked; I didn't feel or see anything. I was hoping it would work for you, too."

I'm shaking my head like this isn't real, like it isn't my life. I'm looking at my mother, but it's as if I'm seeing her for the very first time. She looks so much smaller and frailer than I've ever noticed—head tilted downward, shoulders huddled in—like a little girl herself.

"I'm so sorry, Stacey. I only did what I thought was best."

Tears slide down my cheeks. I look away, remembering how Gram once told me that the more you use your senses, the keener they'll become, but if you decide to push them away, eventually they'll taper off to nothing. No wonder my mother didn't like my close relationship with Gram, didn't like Gram teaching me all she knew about spells and the healing arts. Mom was only trying to protect me.

thirty-four

After breakfast, my mother drops me back off at the dorm, telling me she wants to return to her hotel for a nap and then we'll get together later tonight. I'm still feeling completely stunned and confused by our conversation, but also clearer—if that's even possible.

I storm through the common room with the full intent of relating the details of my life-altering morning to Amber and Drea, swing open the door to our room, and there, standing dead center, gazing into each other's eyes like some cheesy ad for breath-freshening gum, are Chad and Drea. They take a step back when they see me.

"Oh, hi," Drea says, smoothing out the back of her hair. She takes another step away from him, like that will make a difference.

"I came by earlier to see you," Chad says to me.

I manage a nod, noticing how my lip feels like it's trembling.

"But you weren't here," he continues.

Still nodding, doing my best to hold it all together.

"Me and Dray just ended up going for a ride," he says.

"To talk," Drea adds, nodding her head. "We talked."

"What else *would* you be doing?" I ask, almost choking on the words.

"Nothing," Chad says. He looks to Drea, but her gaze has fallen to the floor, to Amber's pile of shoes clumped in the corner. "Whatever you're thinking," he says, "it's not what it looks like."

"And what *does* it look like?"

"Not what you're thinking," he repeats.

"Really?" I say, zooming in on Drea.

She peeks over at me—her cheeks stained with guilt roses—and moves to take a seat on her bunk. "I'm sorry," she says.

Jaw locked, I nod, looking now at Chad, thinking how maybe we've both done our share of romantic line-crossing for one twenty-four–hour period.

"We should talk," Chad says. "About last night."

"I don't have time." I grab the noose, the cassette player, and the letters, and stuff them all into my bag, doing my best to look away so they don't see my face—how upset I must look.

"Where are you off to?" Drea asks.

"I have some stuff to attend to," I say, wiping my eyes. "You know, like saving-my-life stuff?"

"Well, I'm going, too," Chad says.

"Why?"

"What do you mean why? Because I'm worried about you. I heard about that jump-rope thing you got."

"And?"

"And what?"

"Aren't you going to tell me you think it's someone's idea of a prank?"

"Stacey—no."

For just a second, I feel a pang of guilt, jumping to conclusions about his reaction. But then I look at Drea again. She's got her knees scrunched up into her chest, her cheek resting atop them, tears rolling down her face—the picture of sheer and utter heartbreak, which makes me feel even worse.

"I'm gonna go," I say.

"Wait," he says, taking a step toward me, "after last night, you of all people have no reason to be mad at me."

"Nothing happened," I say.

"And nothing happened here," he says. "Can I at least come with you?"

Drea looks up at me for my response.

"My mother's in town," I say. "She just dropped me off for a second to get my stuff. I have to go; she's probably waiting for me now." I feel my lips pucker up at the lie.

"Call me when you get back," he says.

I nod, knowing that I probably will, but also knowing that right now our fighting seems insignificant compared to what could happen within the next couple days. I sling my backpack over my shoulder, a mix of fear, sadness, and re-lief battling inside my heart all at once. I head out to find the one person I'm hoping will be able to put that battle to rest: Jacob.

thirty-five

When I get to the boy's dorm, Mr. What's-his-face, the RD, tells me right away that Chad isn't in his room.

"No," I say, feeling my cheeks pinken. "I'm looking for Jacob."

"Jacob *who?*"

I feel my face go blank. It suddenly occurs to me that I don't know Jacob's last name. "Umm . . ." I stall, "how many Jacobs have you got?"

"Two."

"Well, I'll take the one with the blue hair and dark eyes." Did I just say that? "I mean the *dark* hair and *blue* eyes."

What's-his-face gives me this goofy sort of look—a crooked smile accompanied by dark, furry eyebrows that arch up and down, Amber-style. He picks up the phone and dials Jacob's room to announce my visit. "Mr. *Leblanc* will be down in a jiffy," he says, still ogling at me like this is the age of Puritanism and I'm some scarlet-lettered harlot for wanting to talk to *two* boys in one day.

I mutter a thank-you and look away to avoid his dirty mind. It *is* weird being here, though, looking for someone other than Chad. But when Jacob emerges from behind the double set of doors, that feeling fades. Because I know I'm in the right place. Because I'm confident that he'll be able to help me in some way.

"Hi," he says. "I was hoping we'd see each other today." He's wearing a black turtleneck sweater that shows off a modestly worked chest, and a pair of jeans that hug just enough at the thigh.

I look back at What's-his-face. He's got his chin propped up on his fist, staring at the two of us like we're starring in some cheesy reality dating show, the kind where couples separate to hook up with other people's partners in an effort to test their relationships. Jacob leads me past a few boys scattered around the lobby area—a couple actually studying on a Saturday, a few playing cards, and a group kicking around a Hacky Sack. Since girls aren't allowed in boys' rooms and vice versa, and since he wasn't lucky enough to score one of the more lenient senior houses, we sit at a table in the corner of the lobby where it's relatively private.

"I'm sorry about what happened last night," he says. "If it'll help I can talk to Chad, tell him there isn't anything going on between us."

I search Jacob's eyes a moment, looking for the truth. Maybe it's lost somewhere behind all that grayish-blue, behind the tiny flecks of yellow that spiral the center and aim to suck me in. I mean, does he really mean that? Nothing going on? Wasn't it he who tried to kiss me last night—who got so close to my face and touched my hand and smelled like lemongrass incense and made my insides turn to complete and utter mush? Did all of that *not* happen?

"Forget it," I say, taking a deep and cleansing breath. "Right now I just need your help." I prop my bag up on the table. "I was thinking that maybe we could do a spell together."

He leans back in his chair and looks away. "I don't think so."

"Why?"

"Because spells are kind of private for me. I prefer to do them alone."

"Couldn't you make an exception? I mean, my life is at stake here."

Jacob stares into me for a few seconds without saying a word. A lock of his dark walnut hair falls over one eye, making the stare even more intense, more deliberate. I bite my bottom lip and look away.

"What did you have in mind?" he asks, finally.

I pat over the main section of my bag and release the tooth-grip on my lip. "I thought that maybe we could do something with the noose, maybe try to channel the energy of the person who left it, figure out who it is."

Jacob nods, but I can see his reluctance. I can see it in his eyes and across his lips—a tightish sort of look. He glances off in the direction of the Hacky Sack game. "It's not that I don't want to help you," he says.

"What's the big deal?"

"The big deal?" He looks back at me, a look of surprise hanging on his face. "The big deal is that spells are personal. They reveal things."

"Well, yeah, isn't that the point?"

"No," he corrects. "They reveal personal things—stuff about you, stuff about me, about the people conducting the spells."

"And you don't want that?" I feel myself swallow.

He looks away again. "I don't know."

And I don't even know what I'm asking.

"It's just that I've never had that before," he continues, "that kind of . . . sharing. And I don't know if I'm ready for it now."

"Forget it," I say, feeling my cheeks go pink for the second time today. "I was stupid to even ask." I stand up, sling my bag over my shoulder, and make a beeline for the door.

thirty-six

Instead of going back to the dorm, I hop on the shuttle bus and head into town. I just want to get away right now, even if it's only for an hour. The bus passes by my mother's hotel, prompting me to ring the bell that signals to the driver that I want to get off.

As I make my way through the peach-colored lobby—past couches littered with dandelion-yellow pillows and bud vases filled with bright pumpkin-colored tulips—I think how nice it would be to actually stay here for the week. To shut myself up into some generic room, between four generic walls, and sleep peacefully at night in a big generic bed—to only have to answer to room service and cleaning staff who would remain nameless and faceless throughout my entire, blissful stay.

The person behind the front desk calls my mother's room to announce my visit, and then grants me permission to take the elevator up to the fourth floor. My mother is waiting for me when I get there. Her eyes are heavy, like she's been sleeping, and she's got on a thick terry robe with matching white slippers.

"I'm so glad you stopped by," she says.

She ushers me into the room and I stand in the center, taking it all in—layers of yellow and peach, the shiny, gold-framed prints on the walls, and the long and flowing linen drapes. It's basically an extension of the lobby, only smaller and more compact.

"Would you like something to drink?" she asks, poking her head into the tiny fridge.

"No, thanks," I say, gazing out the window. The clouds have swallowed up the sun and the sky has started to darken. I look at my watch. It's just after four. I wonder if Drea and Amber are looking for me. If Chad and Drea are still together. I clench my teeth at the thought of it, of them, standing there in the middle of our room, almost kissing, and feel my eyes begin to well up all over again.

"Are you hungry?" my mother asks. "Do you want to grab a bite to eat?"

I shake my head and look away. I don't really know what I'm doing here, why I'm not instead back in the room, sucking up whatever personal issues I have with Chad and Drea, and focusing on what's really important. I need to reflect on my dreams so I can piece together what they're trying to tell me, and so I can figure out how the noose, the song, and the mysterious notes fit into the puzzle as well.

But instead I'm here. Because, deep down, after hearing about my mother's experience with dreams and premonitions, I'm hoping she can help me with mine.

"I came to talk," I say, taking a deep and cleansing breath.

She nods like she already knows, and takes a seat on the edge of the bed.

"About my nightmares." I sit down beside her. "That's why you're here, isn't it?"

"I'm here," she says, "because I thought there were some things about me that you should know."

"And now that I know them?"

"What do you mean?"

"I mean, it's horrible what you had to go through. And I'm glad you told me about it. But you also know that I've been having nightmares of my own."

She nods.

"And you know that starting some hobby or joining some club is not going to make them go away. Not now. My senses are too developed."

She turns toward me to place her hand on my shoulder. "You could try if you wanted to, Stacey. If you really put your mind to it, you could train yourself to dream less, to not be able to sense some things. It may take a while, but it could help make your life a lot easier."

"I don't have a while."

"Why? What do you mean?"

"I mean I only have a few days before something horrible is going to happen to me."

"Horrible?"

I nod. "Like what happened to Maura, like what happened to Julia."

My mother clamps her eyes shut, like what I'm saying is no surprise and a complete surprise at the same time—like her worst fears are coming true. "Tell me," she says, her voice all brittle. "What are you dreaming about?"

"Are you going to be all right?" I ask.

More nodding.

"Maybe we should talk tomorrow," I say.

"No." She blots at her eyes with the sleeve of her robe. "You were right when you said I came here because of your nightmares. And so maybe now I just need to put my own to rest."

I sit back down and wrap my arms around her shoulders. Her body is so small against mine, her arms like tiny bird wings, flapping nervously against my back.

"Let's just start from the beginning," she says, "and see what we can figure out."

I spend the next hour or so talking about my Maura and Veronica nightmares, how the Maura nightmares have been making me sick. I tell her about Jacob, how he came here from Colorado because he says he's been having nightmares about me, how he gave me the crystal cluster rock, and how he thinks someone is going to try and strangle me. And then I segue into all the weird stuff I've been receiving.

"So, what you're telling me," she says, "is that the nightmares you were having about Maura four years ago are the same nightmares you're having about her now."

"Not exactly the same," I say. "The only part that's the same is the tool shed. When I was having nightmares about Maura four years ago, I could see her trapped in one."

"And that's where the police ended up finding her body," she says.

I nod. "But now, the nightmares are different. I mean, she's jumping rope, singing weird songs, I'm walking down a corridor in the basement of the school, throwing up all over the place . . . Plus I'm dreaming about Veronica, too. Basically, I'm being haunted by dead people."

My mother shakes her head. "It isn't that easy. You need to remember your nightmares are trying to tell you something—every detail is important."

"So maybe my nightmares are trying to tell me that I'm still feeling guilty about Maura and Veronica."

"Maybe," my mother says, patting at my back. "But deep down you probably already know that's true. No matter how many people you're able to save or how many lives you're able to better, there will probably always be a part of you that will feel you could have done more. It's been that way with me, with Julia's death. I tell myself that it wasn't my fault. And I come here, hoping to make things better by helping you, but that still doesn't change the past . . . or the guilt."

I swallow what she's trying to tell me, but I'm not sure how much I agree with it. I mean, I think there comes a time when you have to forgive yourself for any past wrongs or imperfections. And that helping others does make things better. It doesn't change the past; it doesn't even mask it. But it can help change someone's future.

I rest my head against her shoulder. "So, if it isn't old ghosts haunting me, then what is it?"

"Well," she begins, "your dreams are based on past events. Even that letter you got, asking if you'll keep your promise, implies some promise made in the past."

"Yeah?"

"So maybe you need to go into your past to find the answers."

"Yeah, but my past with Maura couldn't be more different than my past with Veronica Leeman. How do they connect?" I shake my head, wondering if Jacob was right when he said I'm having nightmares about Veronica because she represents death for me, because she represents what can happen if I don't figure all this stuff out.

"Why do you think you've been vomiting?" she asks.

I shrug, thinking how my nightmares last year made me wet the bed and how the bedwetting turned out to be a clue, my body's way of telling me something.

"In your nightmares, are you vomiting out of sickness, like a flu, or is it something else? A food allergy, maybe?"

"Just plain old sickness, I guess," I say, remembering how Jacob said he dreamed about me getting sick as well. But he said it was more like hangover-sickness, like from drinking too much or something.

"Can you think of some reason why that might be happening?" she asks.

I look away, not wanting to remember after so long of just trying to forget—trying to block out all the little details of Maura's death. She had been vomiting too, just minutes before she died.

"Miles Parker," I say.

The thought of him makes me squirm. I can still see his face—close-ups of him on the news going in and out of the courthouse. Reporters shoving their microphones in his face, asking him all sorts of questions about motive—why he took her in the first place, what his intentions were, why he would give a minor alcohol.

"What about him?" my mother asks.

I think back to the details of the trial. When he kidnapped Maura that day, he had picked her up in his car when she was walking home from school—a friendly face from the neighborhood. Only once she got inside the car, she couldn't get back out.

"He had been drinking," I say. "He offered her a 'special drink,' cherry brandy, which made her sick. They found her vomit in his car and on her clothing."

"So, maybe Maura is trying to tell you something," my mother says. "Maybe she's trying to communicate to you through your dreams, maybe to help you in some way."

"Yeah, but what is she trying to say?"

"That's something only you can answer."

We spend the next hour or so hashing and rehashing all the details—until the growling of our stomachs interrupts us. We order room service—plates full of grilled cheese-and-tomato sandwiches, waffle-cut French fries, coleslaw, and butterscotch pudding for dessert. Considering I haven't eaten since this morning's indigestible cheese danish and the few bites of peanut butter pancakes at the diner, and since it's now approaching six, the mix of sugar, fat, and carbs is just what I need.

"You know," my mother says, polishing off what's left in her coffee cup, "I don't know if you remember this, but Gram used to always say that what happens in our past doesn't always stay in the past. It comes out in our present and future."

"What's that supposed to mean?" I lean back on the bed and stare up at the ceiling. "That every horrible tragedy in my life is going to just keep on repeating itself in the future?"

"Maybe when things don't get resolved in the past," she says, "life gives us a second chance to make things right."

"How is saving myself going to make things right for Maura and Veronica?"

"It isn't," she says. "But maybe saving yourself will make things right for *you*."

I spend the next several moments staring up at the ceiling swirls, trying to decipher what all of this means—how saving myself might make things right for me, how the past can come back in our present and future, and why my nightmares are making me sick—what Maura might be trying to tell me, how she might even be trying to help me in some way.

"You still wear Gram's ring," my mother says.

I hold up my hand and look at it—the bright, purpley amethyst stone full of both promise and protection.

"It suits you," she says.

I prop myself up on my elbows. "You really think so?"

She nods and smiles, and I can't help but smile back. It's like she's finally accepting me for who I am and what I believe. I wrap my arms around her and she hugs me back, her wings just a little bit stronger than before.

"I should go. Amber and Drea are probably worried about me."

"Why don't you just stay here tonight?"

"I don't know. Maybe I should get back—face my life, my future."

"Not without a good night's sleep," she says. "Maybe with a little rest, in some place where you feel safe, things will become clearer."

"Maybe," I say.

She touches a strand of my hair where I cut it, as though she can somehow sense my moonlit spell in the woods—the offering I made to the earth in exchange for helping me to see more clearly.

"I think if you want to see more clearly," she begins, "you should really spend some time thinking about the essential things, meditating on them. Only then will you be able to figure out what your past is trying to tell you, why it's come back into your present, and how it will affect your future."

I nod, thinking how now, for the first time ever, she reminds me so much of Gram, after years of thinking they were so completely different.

I end up calling Amber to tell her where I am and that I'll be back first thing in the morning. Amber tells me that Drea wants to talk, but I decline. It's not that I don't want to work things out with her, it's just that I need to do my best to focus on what's essential right now.

thirty-seven

It's extra chilly this morning, but the sun is so bright I decide to take a walk anyway. I head down an unfamiliar street lined with tall, barren trees. There are houses to the left and right—a small suburban neighborhood basically, complete with basketball hoops, minivans, and well-manicured shrubbery.

When I come to the end of the street, I take a left. I notice a grassy field and lots of parked cars. I walk a little farther and see that it's actually a cemetery. There's a crowd of people gathered in a circle around a casket. I feel drawn to it, to them, and feel this weird gnawing in my gut—the need to see whomever it is being lowered down into the ground.

The priest recites a prayer and sprinkles holy water over the casket. I look around at the individual faces. Right up front is a girl who looks just like Donna Tillings. I take a couple steps closer to get a better look. She's dressed all in black and wearing one of those mourning hats, the kind with the net that covers your face. She looks up in my direction and lifts the net so I can see her face. It *is* Donna. She bunches her lips together and then pulls something from her bag, a bouquet of wildflowers. I think she's going to drop them onto the casket, but instead she walks toward me, parting the sea of people in her way.

"I'm glad you came," she says, handing me the bouquet. She kisses me on the cheek and then takes my hand, leading me through the crowd, closer to the casket.

"Who died?" I whisper.

She turns to me, her pasty lips all bunched again, her face scrunched up like she doesn't understand my question. "*You* did," she says. She points down into the casket, the cover flipped open for everyone to see.

I blink my eyes, expecting to see Veronica Leeman, but instead I just see myself. My clothes are the same as the ones I'm wearing right now—black coat, pear-green sweater, baggy jeans, faux Doc Martens. And my hands are folded neatly over my belly, my amethyst ring staring up from my right hand.

"Are you ready?" Donna asks, the rims of her eyes a dark ruby color against such pale skin.

I glance up at the others in the crowd. It seems everyone is waiting for me—Amber and Drea, Chad and Jacob, my mother, Keegan, Trish and Tobias, Cory and Emma; all the cafeteria ladies; Mrs. Halligan, dressed in a seventies blouse with zoo animals; even Mr. What's-his-face, sporting a custodial uniform and a pair of galoshes.

I take a deep breath and look beyond them. I can see someone approaching in the distance. It's Gram. And she's with Maura. They're holding hands like old friends—like they're waiting for me, too. In her other hand, Gram holds a white candle—the same one she gave me on my twelfth birthday. She stops and smiles at me. And Maura blows a giant orange bubble out from her lips.

I take a step toward them, but then Gram shakes her head and I stop. She nods toward the headstone, just to my right. I look at it, at my name etched into the sparkly pink marble. "Here lies Stacey Ann Brown," it reads. "Devoted friend, loving daughter." It has my date of birth engraved just below the inscription, and then today's date.

Today's date.

"Stacey, are you ready?" Donna repeats.

I look back at Gram, at Maura, and then at my mother, and shake my head. "No," I say. "Today is not my day to die."

thirty-eight

I wake up with a start, breathing hard, my heart practically pumping its way through my chest. But I don't feel sick—don't feel that burning urge in the pit of my stomach to lose it all over the place. I suspect it's because my nightmare wasn't completely focused on Maura this time. It was focused more on Veronica Leeman, on the obvious fear I have of ending up just like her.

It's already light outside; I can see the narrow slivers of daylight through the half-shut blinds. My mother has already gotten up. Her side of the bed is empty and the bathroom door is wide open, the light flicked off. So where is she?

I get up as well. I wash my face, brush my teeth, and draw the window drapes wide open, all the while trying to orient myself in the new surroundings. But all I can really think about is the nightmare I just had.

How today is supposedly my day to die.

After a quick shower, I change back into my clothes and knot my hair up in a rubber band. My mother still isn't back yet. I go to make the bed and notice a note lying beside her pillow. It reads:

Dear Stacey,

You were still sleeping but I couldn't stay in bed.
I've gone to the hotel gym, and then I'm going to
find a bakery to get us some fresh croissants
and coffee.

Love, Mom

P.S. I've decided to stay an extra night so we
can have more time together.

She's written the time in the corner of the note—7:45. And now it's after nine. I rush down to the hotel gym to find her, but she isn't there. Nor is she in the locker room. I check the parking lot; her car is gone. I figure she's out coffee-and-croissant shopping, but since time is really of the essence here, I can't afford to wait. I scribble her a message, apologizing for my quick exit but stressing that I really need to get back to campus.

When I get back to the dorm, PJ and Amber are sitting on Amber's bunk.

"How was it with your mom?" Amber asks.

"Good," I say, confident in the reply.

"The phone's been ringing off the hook," she says. "Jacob wants to see you."

"Why?"

"I don't know," Amber says, "but he seems pretty urgent."

"Pant, pant," PJ says.

"What are *you* doing here?" I ask him.

"Freaking out." He plunges his hand into the box of Fruity Pebbles nestled in his lap and stuffs a pile into his mouth.

"Completely freaking," Amber agrees. She lays a hand on his shoulder and he looks away. "He's totally wigged."

"Why?" I take a seat on the edge of my bed. "What's going on?"

"There's some seriously smelly stew brewing up on this campus," Amber says.

"English, please."

"I went to that séance last night," PJ says.

"Great." I fold my arms in front.

PJ rolls his eyes toward the ceiling. "I'm not gonna get into the who, where, and why again with you, Stacey-bee. And how I was really doing this for you. We should be so far beyond that at this point."

"Well, then, what *is* the point?"

"The point is that they're freaking nuts. A freaking can of cashews ready to explode."

"What happened?"

"Can you believe it?" He crosses his legs at the knee. "They only wanted me there to use me."

"Imagine that," I say.

"I mean, I feel so robbed."

"There, there," Amber says, rubbing his forearm.

"So I went," PJ begins. "We met in the basement of the Hangman, a little after eleven last night. Which was fine—late enough for the required spirit-calling ambiance, but early enough so I'd be back before the *Real World* marathon."

"How did you get in?"

"Tobias," he says. "He works there."

"So—"

"So, they only wanted me there to help get Veronica's spirit all wiggy and bothered so she'd do some crazy shit."

"Like what?"

"You know . . . blink the lights, shatter the windows, take over someone's body and make them chant verse in Latin?"

"And did those things happen?"

He shakes his head and crams his mouth with another fistful of cereal. The whole picture of it, of him, so freaked out, chain-eating Fruity Pebbles like some cereal junkie, tells me there's much more to it.

"They wanted me," he says between chews, "since they knew Veronica and I didn't exactly see nose to nose on things."

"Or eye to eye," Amber corrects.

"They want to reenact that night," PJ continues.

"What night?"

"You know," he says, his eyes all big from fright. "*That* night. In O'Brian? In the French classroom? You, walking down the hallway, calling out her name? Veronica's body sprawled out on the floor, prune juice running from her hair . . ."

"Blood," Amber whispers.

"The night Donovan killed her?" I say.

"Is there another night that matches that description?" he asks, frustration high in his voice.

"Why are they doing this?" I ask.

He shakes his head. "Because they're messed. Because they're obsessed with what happened last year. They see Veronica as some sort of twisted idol, victimized by her peers. They seem to think she's looking for revenge, and they want to help her get it."

"Cory and Tobias have actually been in contact with Donovan," Amber says.

"What?" I feel my chest constrict; my lower lip trembles. I bite at the quivering—a meager effort to try and retain some sort of control.

"They've been brainstorming ways to get him out of that juvenile detention center," Amber says.

"So he can participate in the reenactment." PJ swallows hard and makes a face, like he's just ingested a spoonful of sludge.

"But they haven't been successful," I say. "I mean, you can't just break someone out of one of those places. Right?"

"I don't know," PJ says, chewing on the tips of his fingers now. "They had all sorts of letters from him. They wouldn't show me everything, not until I proved my loyalty."

"And how are you supposed to prove that?" I ask.

"By getting *you* there."

"Me?"

He nods. "Tonight—for the reenactment."

thirty-nine

We end up talking to PJ about the whole séance incident for another half-hour or so. Just until Drea comes in.

"I need to talk to you." She sits down next to me on the bed. Her normally perfectly pouted lips are now more grimaced, and her aura's a dreary olive color. She stares down at her shoes—melon-peach sneakers to match her scarf—and then peeks at me.

"Okay," I say, even though I know I don't have much time.

We move outside, onto the front steps where it's quiet, and sit there a few moments, just looking out at the lawn.

"I'm sorry about what happened yesterday morning," she says finally. "You know, when you came in and I was with Chad."

"What *did* happen?"

She shakes her head. "Nothing, really."

"Then why do you need to apologize?"

"Because maybe I wanted something to happen."

"Oh."

She turns to face me. "I'm still in love with him, Stacey."

I clamp my eyes shut and look away, feeling her words burn straight through my heart.

"I'm sorry. I can't help it. I've tried. I've told myself that he's yours, that you're the one who's with him now. That I'm over him. But I'm not. I still love him. I think I always will."

I bite my lip and stare down at my hands, at the chapped skin on my palms. I feel a nest of tears hatch behind my eyes. I knew it would only be a matter of time before Drea and I had this conversation. It's just . . . I wasn't prepared for it to happen now, in the middle of everything, when I need more than ever for the constants in my life to stay just that—constant.

"Say something," she says, looking away.

"What do you want me to say?"

A part of me wants to ask her if Chad feels the same, but I can't, because I'm not sure I could handle the answer right now.

"Have you told Chad how you feel?" I ask.

She shakes her head. "But I think he knows. I think he's always known."

I nod because I know she's right. Because she *does* love Chad. Maybe even more than I do. "So what now?"

"I don't know. I don't know what he's thinking. Sometimes I feel like he feels the same, you know? But then he sees you and I feel like everything changes."

I sink back against the step and take a breath, thinking how this whole scene feels so familiar, how it was just last year that I put her through this exact same thing. And then I think how oddly okay I feel I am going to be about it, how maybe I've sensed it all along—that Chad and I aren't meant to be together, not the way the two of them are.

"Just tell me you don't hate me," she says.

I manage to look at her neck, at the brownish mole on her chin, and then up into her eyes. She's crying, too. There's a trickle of tears running down her cheek. "I don't hate you," I say, wiping away the last of my tears.

And I don't hate her. I can't. Even though a part of me wants to.

forty

After my talk with Drea, I nurse my wounds as best I can with a few breaths of lavender, a couple dabs of patchouli oil behind my ears and at the front of my neck, and several droplets of rose water at my temples. I tell myself that it's good that Drea is being honest with me—because maybe it's forcing me to be honest with myself. This coupled with the aromatherapy recipe I've got swimming on my skin, helps center me a bit—helps me refocus on the essential.

I take a deep breath and return one of Jacob's many phone calls. He tells me he's reconsidered joining forces to do a spell and wants me to come to his room ASAP. I don't stop to ask him how he plans to sneak me inside. Instead I just hang up, grab the noose, the letters, and the cassette player, and cram a bunch of random spell supplies—a handful of vanilla beans, sandwich bags full of dried basil and dill, and a tiny bottle of sesame oil—into my backpack.

When I get to his dorm, he's standing outside, waiting for me. "I've got everything ready in my room," he says. "But you need to wait here until I can get rid of the RD."

I wait several minutes until Jacob signals to me that it's safe to go in. He ushers me through the lobby, up a couple flights of stairs, and down a narrow hallway. We end up passing by a few boys along the way—freshmen mostly, I think—who give me weird looks, ogling me extra hard like they've never seen a girl before.

Jacob's room is the last door on the left. He unlocks it and we go in. A typical boys' room. Posters of classic rock bands line the walls—the Beatles, the Doors, the Police. There are also dirty clothes piled high on the floor, neutral shades of coffee and blue, and the requisite *Sports Illustrated* swimsuit calendar thumbtacked to a bulletin board.

"My roommate's a slob," he says, closing the door behind us. "This is mostly all his stuff."

"Where is he?" I ask, looking toward the spell supplies gathered on what is obviously Jacob's bed.

"Out. He's always out. I barely ever even see the guy."

I nod, taking note of how nervous Jacob seems. He fumbles with his keys, dropping them once before managing them inside his pocket.

"Was it hard to get rid of the RD?" I ask, hoping to lighten the tension.

Without so much as glancing in my direction, he kicks a clear pathway through the piles of clothes on the floor leading to his bed. "Not really. I just told him one of the toilets on the first floor overflowed."

"Did it?"

He nods. "Thanks to a pair of briefs."

"Lovely," I say.

"Tell *him* that. I just hope he has a pair of galoshes handy." Jacob folds his arms and looks over the spell supplies sprawled out over a cranberry-colored square of fabric that takes up half the bed.

"I brought some spell stuff of my own," I say, unzipping the main compartment of my backpack.

"I have everything," he says.

"How about the noose and the letters and stuff?" I ask, ready to take them out.

He shakes his head. "We have all we need right here."

"What are we going to do?" I ask, taking a seat on the corner of his bed.

"I'd like to do a spell that focuses on your past. I'm thinking between your dreams about Maura and the letter, referring to some past promise, that that's where the answer lies."

"That's funny," I say. "My mother said the same thing."

He nods, almost like he knows.

"So where do we start?" I ask

Jacob turns to light a stick of incense. That's when I notice the chunky white candle sitting atop his night table. It looks exactly like mine.

"You have a white candle," I say.

"You seem surprised."

"It's just that it looks like one my grandmother gave me, that's all."

He swallows hard and turns around to face me.

"Are you going to light it?" I ask.

"No."

"Why?" I swallow.

He's looking at me so purposefully, almost through me, like he can see right into my soul. "Because it's not time."

"Then when will be the time?"

"Don't you know?" he asks. "White is for magic."

I feel my lower lip quiver, just hearing my grandmother's words come from his mouth. "How do you know that?"

"What do you mean? Don't you think so, too?"

"I don't know. I mean, that's what my grandmother said it meant."

He nods like he understands completely, like this comes as no shock at all.

"But that doesn't make sense," I continue. "I mean, why does there have to be some special time to light a white candle? We do magic all the time. At least *I* do."

Jacob smiles like he can sense my frustration. "Magic is more than just spells, don't you think? We'd be cheating ourselves so much if that's all we thought it was."

"No," I say. "I know there's more to it." And I do know there's more—like the magical elements of spirit and nature; like the moon, casting its light when you need to see. But I still don't understand what my grandmother was trying to tell me.

"True magic," he says, "encompasses so much. It encompasses all the wonderful little things that can't be explained—pure things."

I nod, still waiting for the light to click on in my head.

"So, maybe your grandmother wanted you to wait until you experienced some specific aspect of magic before you lit that candle."

"Like what?"

Jacob turns away to arrange a group of rocks on his desk. "Like love," he says, his voice low, like there's a part of him that doesn't want me to hear.

Love? I gulp at the thought.

"At least that's what my uncle told me to wait for before lighting mine."

"Your uncle?"

He nods, gathering the rocks up into a clump. "My uncle and I were close growing up. He was really the only one I could relate to."

"And he's the one who gave you the candle?"

Jacob turns around to face me again. He nods, his cheeks a little flushed. "On my twelfth birthday."

I feel myself start to tremble. My heart quickens inside my chest, stirring up my nerves, rattling through my bones. I fold my arms and broaden my stance in an effort to regain composure. I wonder if he can sense it—how shaken I am, how much alike we both are.

"Anyway," he says, taking a deep breath to change the subject, "before we begin the spell, there needs to be complete trust."

"Trust?" My head is spinning.

He nods. "In order to combine our energies on any spell, in order for it to work, we have to be able to trust one another completely."

"Okay," I say.

"Not okay," he corrects. "Because I know you don't trust me completely."

I open my mouth to object, but I can't. Because there is this tiny place inside me that's holding back from trusting him completely. "Trust has always been a tough one for me."

"It's okay," he says. "Because I don't completely trust you either."

What? I mean, after all this time I've spent questioning him and his motives, reasons why he'd pack up his life and move all the way across the country, it just never dawned on me—the possibility that *he* didn't trust *me.*

"If I trusted you completely," he begins, "I wouldn't have hesitated when you asked me to do a spell together. I told you spells are private for me. I've never shared them with anyone."

"So what are we even doing here?" I ask. "If you don't think a collaborative spell will work—"

"I didn't say it *wouldn't* work." Jacob sits down beside me on the bed. "I only said it wouldn't work if we didn't trust each other."

"So how are we supposed to trust each other now?"

He motions to the spell supplies. "That's what this stuff is for. Before we do a spell that focuses on your past, we need to do one that bonds us together with trust."

"Spells don't create trust," I say, standing up.

"This one will." He stands up as well, landing smack dab in front of my face—eye-to-eye, lip-to-lip. He smells like coconut oil.

I feel my lip tremble and I think he sees it, too. The corners of his mouth curl slightly upward, as if to smile.

"Maybe we should get started then," I say, stepping back. I sit back down on the bed and begin fumbling with a squarish jar of some sort. "What do we do first?"

Jacob plugs a hot plate into the wall by his desk. "We're going to make body paint."

"Body paint?"

He pulls a tank top from the top drawer of his dresser and tosses it to me. "So you won't get your clothes dirty."

"I'm supposed to wear this?"

He nods and pulls another tank top out for himself.

"I don't think so."

"This is what I'm talking about," he says. "You need to trust me." He takes a step toward me and reaches for my hand. "I have as much to lose in this as you do."

"Your life isn't at stake," I say.

"No," he says. "But yours is." His slate-blue eyes penetrate mine so deeply I have to look away. "I'll turn around and you can change over there." He nods toward the corner of the room.

As soon as he turns around, I move in that direction, just to the right of the door, thinking how if I wanted to, I could just walk out.

But of course I don't.

I pull my sweater over my head and slip the tank top on over my bra, reminding myself that I still have a boyfriend, that I shouldn't be feeling this way, that there are far more pressing things to concern myself with at the moment.

The tank hangs down mid-thigh and smells like him, like coconut oil and lemongrass incense. It droops a bit low under my arms, revealing the sides of my bra. I tuck the fabric of the tanktop into the spandex and turn to glance at myself in the mirror—at my long, dark hair, at my golden-brown eyes and angular cheeks. The tank top hugs a bit at the chest and hips and makes my skin look lighter in color, almost creamy. And for some inexplicable reason, standing here on a mound of sweatpants mixed with T-shirts, in his clothes, in his room, under these conditions, I couldn't feel more . . . beautiful.

"Okay," I say, almost eager for him to see me, to see this part of me. But instead he just pulls off his shirt and changes into a tank as well.

I look away, feeling a swell of heat move down the length of my spine, thinking how Chad used to make me feel this way, how that seems so long ago, now.

"Okay," he says. "All set." The tank hugs just slightly around his chest, showing off the tops of his arms, like balls of muscle beneath the skin. I allow him to look at me as well; I wonder how he sees me, what I look like to him—a friend, a girl with a boyfriend, a puzzle he has yet to solve.

"Let's get started," he says, ever respectful, keeping focused on my eyes. He takes the ceramic pot from the center of the scarf and holds it out to me. There's an olive-green powder inside, like colored flour, but it smells more like hay. "Have you ever used henna before?"

I shake my head.

"It's perfect for body paint." He pours a small pitcher of liquid into the pot. "Rainwater," he explains. And then he adds in a couple tablespoons of instant coffee, a few squeezes of a lemon, eucalyptus oil, honey, cardamom, and a cinnamon stick.

He mixes it all up with a wooden spoon and then sets the pot on the hot plate. "It'll only be a few minutes," he says. "Heating it up this way just allows the paint to darken."

I look inside the pot as he stirs, watching the liquid swallow up the greenish powder. The ingredients fold into the mix like watered-down cake batter, turning everything a darkish-brown. "It almost looks good enough to eat," I say.

"That means it's ready." He takes the pot by the handle and sets it on a ceramic dish.

"What are we going to do?" I ask, like it isn't obvious.

"First," he says, "we need to focus on what we already know about the impending danger, and then we need to ask ourselves what we'd *like* to know."

"The what-we'd-like-to-know part seems pretty obvious," I say.

"Is it really, though?" He continues to mix the body paint with the wooden spoon and then dips his finger into the center. "Just right."

"Of course it's obvious," I say, getting back to the subject. "I want to know who's been sending me stuff, who's watching me, and what's going to happen to me exactly."

"I'll bet you already know the answers to some of those questions." He holds up his index finger, an ample helping of thick, brown body paint on the tip. "Are you ready?"

"For what?" I ask, leaning back.

"If we're going to build trust, we need to paint on each other. We need to physically show one another what we know, what we desire to know . . . We need to be vulnerable to one another."

"You're kidding, right? Since when will painting on another person's body parts make one vulnerable to anything?"

Jacob looks a bit dejected by my response, which makes me feel like a megabitch. I don't know what is wrong with me sometimes. I've had Amber and Drea engage in plenty of seemingly bizarre spell stunts. Plus, wasn't it me who buried a potato just the other day? Who made a wax doll and slept with him under my pillow? So why should I have a problem with this?

With his muddied finger, Jacob draws a spiral in the center of his palm—one with five layers and that extends toward his wrist.

I dip my finger into the body paint as well and draw a spiral that matches his. I hold my palm out to him as a peace offering. "Shall we start over?"

Jacob hesitates but then places his palm up against mine, the heat from his hand penetrating right into my own. "There's just one rule," he says.

"What's that?"

"Henna stains big time, so you have to be sure about the images that you draw—purposeful about them."

"Deal."

I pull up my hair in a rubber band, and we spend the next several minutes drawing down each other's arms, at the back of each other's necks, and, pulling up the tanktops, on each other's backs. I draw the noose on his forearm; the letter M where the back of his neck meets his shoulders; the words I'M WATCHING YOU down his left bicep; and the weathered gray basement door from my nightmares on his back, just above his waist.

Jacob does the same on me. I can feel lines and swirls being formed along my shoulders and at the nape of my neck as he parts my hair. Triangular shapes and checkered patterns under my arms, tickling me, giving me goosebumps. I wonder if he can see my bra, if he notices the heat I'm sure is visible all over my face.

Jacob turns me around so that we face one another, his finger raised high to draw. He takes a step inward; we're standing so close now I can feel his breath on my forehead. Jacob looks at me so intensely that I almost want to make a joke, release the tension around us. I feel myself swallow, feel my lower lip quiver, just inches from his mouth. He lowers his finger to my front, right beside one of the tank straps. He looks at me to make sure I'm okay and then draws something that extends across my collarbone, just below my neck and close to the opposite shoulder. At first I try to figure out what it might be, but then I sort of lose track of the lines.

"Are you ready to go on with the spell?" Jacob asks. "Do you trust me yet?"

"Do you?" I ask.

Jacob leans in even closer, still looking at me, into my eyes. His breath is warm on my skin and smells like cinnamon sticks and honey—like the paint. "Do you really have to ask?"

I shake my head slightly and the tips of our noses touch. I close my eyes and lightly rest my forehead against his. Jacob runs his hands down the length of my bare arms; I do the same, moving my fingers along the nape of his neck, enjoying the smell of the paint on each other's skin, the way the stickiness feels under my fingertips.

Jacob stops a moment to move my hair off my shoulders. He looks at me and I close my eyes, feel his mouth on mine, sending a million tiny tingles all over my skin. His kiss is like warm honey and mocha on my tongue, only better, like nothing I've ever quite tasted.

I wrap my arms around him completely, feeling his shoulder blades through the tank top, the shaved hair at the nape of his neck. I open my eyes for a moment and glance over his shoulder at the white candle sitting by his bed and a gush of emotion comes over me all at once—how I've never felt this way before. I mean, *this* way—the way my heart has swelled up inside my chest, like it couldn't get any bigger, the way I'd love to just crawl up inside his skin and breathe his breath.

The way I'd give anything right now to light that white candle.

"Are you thinking what I'm thinking?" he asks.

"I think so," I say.

That's when the door flies open, breaking the moment, slicing through our embrace.

I let out a gasp.

It's Tobias.

"What's going on in here?" he asks, his left eye twitching at us.

"This is my roommate," Jacob explains, taking a step away from me.

"Sorry," Tobias says, "didn't mean to interrupt anything scandalous. Just wanted to pick up a couple of my things." He looks about the room, picks a baseball cap off the floor, and sets it on his head. "So, what *did* I interrupt, exactly?"

"You live with *him*?" I say, turning to Jacob.

"Maybe I should go," Tobias says. "Don't want to get in the middle of anything . . . sticky."

"No," I say, "I'm the one who's leaving."

"So soon?" Tobias asks. "Why? Is Chad waiting for you?"

"Don't go," Jacob says.

I can't believe this is happening. I glance at myself in the mirror, at the picture of what Tobias is seeing. That's when I notice—what Jacob has drawn at my front.

"I have to go." I grab my sweater and bullet for the door before either of them can stop me.

forty~one

When I get back to the room, no one's there. I pull off my
sweater and stand in front of the mirror, looking over all of
Jacob's drawings—a moon, a set of keys, a giant X (the rune
for partnership), and a smallish structure of some sort,
maybe the tool shed from my nightmare since there's a
hammer just below it. But the drawings that disturb me the
most are the ones on my chest—a crudely drawn car, a tree,
and a stick-figured girl jumping rope.

I sit down on the edge of my bed and try to piece it all together. It's all becoming clear now—just like my mother said. The answers to what I need to know are in my past.

When Maura told Miles that she wanted to get out of the car that day, he got angry and started driving faster, taking more turns, making Maura more nervous, more sick. It wasn't long before the car crashed into a tree. Maura flew through the windshield. The doctors said she didn't die right away. Miles, with barely even a scratch, panicked and ended up carrying her body through the woods, just a couple blocks from our neighborhood. He locked her up in a tool shed instead of taking her to the hospital where she could have been saved.

It was a few days before her body was found, and by that time it was too late. She was already dead. Without any past criminal record, Miles was charged with motor vehicle homicide, the kind where they say negligence is to blame, and sentenced to seven to ten years in prison, eligible for parole in four.

Four years ago last month.

I clasp my stomach and massage my throat, feeling the sensation to get sick as well. To vomit, just like Maura, just like my nightmares.

I fish into my spell drawer for a rag and a bottle of olive oil. I douse the rag with the oil and then wipe the henna stains from my neck, chest, shoulders, and arms. The designs begin to lift and lighten a bit. I pull on a turtleneck sweater to cover it all up and then grab the bowl of lavender pellets by my bed. I rub them between my fingers, breathing the scent in, trying to soothe myself.

I wonder what all of this means, if Miles is already out. Or maybe someone knows about all of this; maybe someone, even Jacob himself, found out all these pieces of my life—researched all my old ghosts—and is using them to try and drive me insane. There are certainly plenty of losers around here who have researched the events of last year, who have tried to pry into my life. But is that even possible? Could Jacob have found out all the details of Miles' trial? Is he maybe working with Cory and them?

My head fuzzes over with questions. I lie back on my bed to try and think through at least a few of them. I'm pretty sure the letter *M* is for Maura—at least that's what I sensed in my nightmare when I saw her drawing it. Like jumping rope and singing, drawing on the sidewalk with crayons was just one of the things that Maura liked to do. I'm also pretty sure that the words to the "Miss Mary Mack" song were distorted per Amber's baby corn theory—that it's my mind's way of telling me that I'm scared, twisting things around to create the worst, most frightening possible scenario, something straight out of a Freddie Krueger movie.

But what I still want to know is why anyone would want to cause harm to me. Why would someone go through all the trouble of researching my past? What do they really have to gain from it? And then I remember something I had tried to block out.

The letter.

I sit up in bed, the memory rushing at me all at once. I wrote a letter to Miles Parker just days after the sentencing. An angry letter from a tormented, guilt-ridden thirteen-

year-old girl, telling him how angry I was about that pa-
thetic sentence, how I had sensed all along that she had
been kidnapped, that the person who did it had hidden her
away in a tool shed. I told him how I'd have to live with the
guilt of knowing all this and not doing anything about it for
as long as I lived.

And then I promised him something in the last line of the
letter. I promised that when he got out I'd come after him,
to make him pay—to see that justice was finally served.

Is that the promise referred to in the letter I got?

I pick up the phone to call someone, anyone . . . my
mother at her hotel. But the person at the front desk tells
me she isn't in her room. I hang up and bury my head in
my hands. My forehead is pounding. I want to be sick. I try
sipping some ginger ale, but that just makes it worse.

I rush into the bathroom just in time, before the contents of my stomach empty out into the toilet bowl. I sit
back on my heels and hear myself sob out loud. Because
this is so confusing. Because I don't know where else to
turn or whom I can trust. I look down at my amethyst ring,
wishing my grandmother were here to help me. Wishing
my mother were by my side right now.

forty-two

Instead of feeling better, the urge to be sick remains thick in my throat. And my head still aches—a throbbing pain that makes everything else feel heavy and cold. I set a warm compress over my forehead and lie down in bed, the covers up over my shoulders to stifle the chill.

I close my eyes, which eases me a bit. Maybe a little sleep, even for just a few minutes, will do me some good, will help put things into perspective.

But a few minutes turn into several hours. I wake up to the sound of the phone ringing. I spring up; the warm compress, now cool, drops from my forehead. I don't even think I moved once in my sleep. There's a wrapped sandwich and a bag of chips from the cafeteria at the foot of my bed. I smile, knowing that either Amber or Drea, or both, are looking after me.

The phone continues to ring. I lean over to reach for it, noticing that my headache has subsided a bit, that my stomach has eased some.

"Hello?"

"Hello, Stacey," says a whispery male voice.

"Who is this?"

"We have Drea."

"*What?*"

"You heard me. And if you don't do exactly what I say, she'll be dead."

I almost can't believe what I'm hearing. It's like a bad horror flick come to life. I can tell there's a rag held over the receiver to muffle the sound, so I can't quite recognize the voice.

"*Who is this?*" I repeat.

"You'll find out when you get here."

"Tell me who this is or I'm calling the police."

"Do that and Drea will die," the caller says.

"How do I know you really have her?" I ask.

"How do you know that I don't?"

I glance over at Drea's bed; it's just how she left it this morning.

"Come to the O'Brian building at eleven tonight," the caller continues. "Enter the building through the window of room 104 and then go to the French room."

"Is this Cory?" I ask, glancing at the clock. It's just after nine.

"Stacey, just do what he says." It's Drea's voice.

"Drea?"

"I told you I had her." The whispery male voice comes back on the phone. "And if you call the police, she'll be dead. Just like Veronica Leeman."

The phone clicks as he hangs up. I hang up, too. I know this must have something to do with Cory and Tobias and their séance. They want me to go to the scene of the crime, at the precise time that it happened, so they can re-create the night Veronica died, just like PJ warned. They've kidnapped Drea because it was probably the only way they could think of to get me over there on the anniversary of Veronica's death. Plus, it sort of works for the whole re-creating-the-scene thing, seeing that Donovan kidnapped Drea shortly after he killed Veronica.

I pick up the phone and dial PJ's number, looking for Amber, hoping maybe PJ can help me in some way. But he isn't there. I hang up and call Chad. Not there either. I try Jacob's line but get a busy signal. I slam the phone down, panic starting to set in. I seriously contemplate calling campus police, but I don't. Because I don't want to risk it. I can't. Not now. Not tonight.

I grab the crystal cluster rock and my sachet of thyme for courage and mentally prepare myself to head over to the O'Brian building—to find Drea and put an end to this whole séance fiasco once and for all. I've left a note for Amber telling her where I've gone, and I've left phone messages for Chad and PJ. I have no idea where everyone is tonight; I just know I can't wait around. If today is supposed to be my day to die, I'd better get started changing the future. I'll just have to rescue Drea along the way.

.   .   .

I stuff a flashlight into my bag and close and lock the door behind me, stopping just long enough to look up at the clock—9:30. The caller said to get there at eleven, but I have no intention of playing by his screwed-up rules.

I decide to take the bike path behind our dorm since it cuts a few minutes off the hike over to the main buildings. And just as soon as I start walking, I hear someone following behind me, the sound of footsteps—hard boot heels, I think—clomping toward me on the pavement. I stop. I glance back. But I don't see anything and I no longer hear anyone.

I turn back around and clasp the crystal in my pocket, reminding myself of its protective energy, doing my best to distract myself from what could very well be normal, everyday paranoia. I breathe the night air in, noticing how frigid it is tonight. The sky is an icy black color, like it could crack open at any second and sprinkle down a helping of snow. I knot the knitted scarf around my neck and fold my arms in front, the crystal still gripped in my palm.

The footsteps start up again. I quicken my pace and the person following does the same. Faster now, the pathway narrows a bit through the brush, making it darker, colder, more confining.

I focus on the area ahead of me—the back parking lot of the library is just ahead. I quicken my pace even more, until I'm running, until I can no longer hear the person behind me. Finally, I come to the end of the path—it spits out into the parking lot—and look around for someone, anyone . . . a police cruiser, maybe. I turn to glance back toward the path, but it's too dark, too laden with brush. I clench the crystal in my palm to temper the shaking inside me, the pounding of my heart. Then I cut across the parking lot and move around to the front of the library.

There's a couple of underclassmen standing outside, laughing it up over some stupid joke; I couldn't be more happy to see them, to see anyone. I'm thinking they sense my fear. They stop to watch me as I bound up the steps, three at a time, my face twisted as though I might cry out at any moment—I can feel it on my lips.

Breathing hard, I make it through both sets of double doors and turn to gaze out toward the front of the building. No one. Just the same kids, still watching me, probably wondering what's wrong.

I go to the on-campus phone on the wall and try calling Chad, but I get his voice mail again. I call our room. More voice mail. And Jacob's line is still busy. I hang up and peek back out toward the front of the building. The underclassmen have left and I can't seem to spot anyone else. I move out onto the front steps and gaze up at the O'Brian building, set back a bit from the other buildings. Or at least it feels that way—darker, quieter, more secluded.

I take a giant breath and make my way back out, past the tennis court, and onto the pathway that leads to the building. This time I feel like I'm alone. The footsteps that followed before are no longer with me; maybe it was just my imagination.

This is what I tell myself, anyway, with each step that brings me closer to the building. It's so weird being back here, walking across the lawn that surrounds it, remembering how it was only a year ago that I sat behind Veronica Leeman in French class—her starchy, hair-spray-glued hair resting in a clump on my desk whenever she slouched down in her seat—only a year ago that I found her dead on that same classroom floor.

I swallow the ball of fear in my mouth and walk around the side of the building by the soccer field. I didn't think it would be this hard. I mean, sure, I see the building on a regular basis—I have to pass by it to go to classes, have to see it out of the corner of my eye on my way to the library or on walks across campus. But I mostly try to avoid it—try to look the other way or hold my breath until it's out of sight. Plus, this feels much different. Tonight, I have to go in.

I take the flashlight from my bag and move around to the back of the building, passing the window of room 104, looking for some other opening. I know exactly why the caller wanted me to come in that way. It's because that's the window I entered last year when I went to save Veronica; when instead of saving her, I ended up finding her already dead.

I'm so sure it's one of them who's taken Drea—Cory and his clones—bound on some ridiculous mission to raise

Veronica from the dead, to re-create a scene they've been obsessing about, probably since it first struck the news.

It's much darker back here, the spotlights that shine at the front and sides of the building too shallow to reach behind it. I aim my light toward the windows and doors, wondering if there might be another way in, hoping Cory and them don't see the flashlight beam. I stop when I notice that one of the windows is open a crack. I take a deep breath and peer over my shoulder. I don't see anyone—just the wooded acreage that surrounds the campus. But being back here, in almost complete darkness, I can't shake the feeling that someone's watching me. I take a few steps closer to the window, feeling now more than ever that there's no turning back.

forty-three.

Using the soft beam of the flashlight to direct me, I hoist myself up onto the window sill and crawl through, the hard rubber soles of my shoes smacking down against the linoleum flooring. I aim the beam around the perimeter of the room. It's Señora Sullivan's Spanish room. There are bits of Spanish-speaking culture still alive on the walls— magazine cutouts of tortillas and frijoles, maps of Peru and

Argentina, and, as though by fate, a giant poster of *el Dia de los Muertos*, the Day of the Dead.

I head toward the door at the front of the room. It's just after ten. I still have almost an hour before they're expecting me—an hour to find Drea and get the hell out of here before we both end up as pawns in their game.

Or before I end up dead.

I carefully wrap my hand around the doorknob and twist. The door squeaks slightly as I pull it open, but what cements me in place is the thumping noise coming from just outside the window where I entered. I quickly click my flashlight off and wait a few moments. The thumping stops, like whoever is out there can sense my suspicion.

I clench the sachet of thyme in my pocket and step out into the hallway. It's completely dark except for the few glowing exit signs at both ends of the building. I suspect Cory and his friends are already here, probably getting things ready for their big night. I just wonder where they have Drea.

The flashlight gripped in my hand, I do my best to navigate my way down the main corridor, toward the French room, without having to use it. I'm pretty sure no one can see me in such darkness; I'm just hoping no one will hear me as well. I feel like it's so loud inside my head right now— my heart pumping, my stomach clenching, a screaming sensation behind my eyes.

I step on something that breaks my concentration, making me jump. I step again. It's soft beneath my feet. I scoot down to feel what it is. A cloth of some sort, like a tarp for painting. I reach out and feel the space around me—a couple cans of paint, I think; a few paint rollers; some rags. And a rope.

My heart starts pounding, thrashing inside my chest because I know just what it is. I swallow hard and inch my grip down the length until I feel it—them. Handles.

A jump rope.

I clamp my hand over my mouth to stop the screaming inside my head. Why are they doing this? How do they know? A whimper escapes from my throat. I do my best to crawl free of everything without making any more noise.

Voices come from the end of the hallway—whispery voices that I can't identify. I wrestle myself up and move toward them, past the main entrance and now clearly back on linoleum flooring.

There's a scratching sound just to the right of me—an amplified scratching, like the sound is emanating from a speaker. I stop. My heart wallops inside my chest.

"Hello, Stacey," says the voice from the loudspeaker. *His* voice.

Donovan.

"Welcome back," he says.

My chin shakes. My knees soften. I feel my head start to spin, like my world could come crashing down at any moment.

"I'm watching you," he says.

Still paralyzed in place, it's everything I can do not to cry out, not to switch on the flashlight and surrender to my fate. But I can't. Not now. Not with Drea depending on me.

I move farther down the hallway. The French room is just a few yards away now. I slowly approach the doorway, visions of Veronica Leeman lying dead on the floor heavy on my mind—the pool of blood surrounding her head; the clay planter, what Donovan hit her with, still intact on the floor beside her.

My mouth fills up with fear—a sour, salty paste at the base of my tongue that makes me want to heave. I take a deep breath and stand just to the right of the French room door, mentally readying myself to peer in. From this angle, I can see candles lit at the back of the room. I take a step closer. More candles—a circle of them in the middle of the floor, designating perhaps the sacred space for the séance.

I'm just about to click on my flashlight, to see if there's any sign of Drea, when I notice a few candles move at the front of the room. They're lighting the faces of Emma and Trish, who hold them midair and whisper back and forth about tonight's plans, how Veronica's spirit will tell them what to do.

The scratching sound begins again on the loudspeaker. "Hello, Stacey," Donovan's voice repeats.

"Is she even here yet?" Emma asks.

"It's only 10:15." Trish moves to the sacred circle and takes a seat at the head.

I step back into the hallway and press my spine up against the wall, as though the darkness alone isn't enough to conceal me, as though the wall has the power to swallow me up whole. I do my best to breathe in and out, to calm this pumping in my chest, and to hold it together, when all I really want to do is fall apart.

My only hope is that Amber, Chad, and PJ have gotten my message by now, that they've done the sensible thing and called campus police, that they're on their way.

forty-four

My back still pressed up against the wall, I can hear someone walking at the other end of the hallway; their footsteps
squeak against the linoleum floor and echo off the walls.
I'm pretty sure the person's alone, pretty sure they're
headed this way, to the French room. But I'm also pretty
sure that this isn't the same person who was following me
from the dorm earlier. Those footsteps made a clomping
sound, like from boot heels; these are definitely sneakers.

A flashlight beam shines down in this direction. I look toward the exit lights to my right. There's a set of doors there, but whoever is approaching will probably be able to see me leave.

The beam gets closer and so do the footsteps—past the main entrance now, on this side of the building. I can hear people moving in the French room, probably hearing the approaching footsteps as well.

I step quickly past the open doorway and stand mid-hallway. I can't stay here; I know the flashlight beam will eventually make its way to me, catch me like a deer in headlights. Or Emma and Trish's candles will be just enough to cast a shadow over my hiding body.

"Stacey," the loudspeaker crackles. "I'm watching you."

I step across the hallway and slip into a classroom. I crouch down behind the door and wait. My heart is beating so loud and fast I think it must be audible. I ball myself up tighter, my knees pressed into my chest, and hold my breath.

After what seems like several minutes of not hearing anything else, I inch my way from behind the door and remain crouched in the doorway. The flashlight beam is gone and everything seems vacant. I crawl toward the double doors and feel something beneath my fingertips. A stick of some sort. I feel around on the ground a bit more and find more of them. I pick one up and run my fingertip over the smooth, buttery tip, the paper wrapped around it.

They're crayons.

I swallow down the jittering inside me as best I can and push the doors ever so slightly. They make a moaning noise, but, as though by some wonderful and all-knowing force, the scratching sound plays again over the loudspeaker and manages to drown it out—just enough for me to crawl through the crack I've made.

I click on my flashlight and move as quickly and quietly as possible down a set of stairs. Another pair of exit doors faces me, the ones that will lead me outside. I go to dive right through them, to run and get help. But it's like I'm frozen in place, nailed to the floor. I'm going to be sick. I hold the quake in my stomach, the juices gurgling, climbing their way up to my throat. What does this mean? What is this sickness trying to tell me?

My head is throbbing, trying to make sense of everything. I take another step toward the exit doors and my mouth fills with the warmest, most pungent sour taste—like my body won't let me leave. Like I have no choice but to go with my instincts.

I turn to gaze down another flight of stairs. And that's when I know—when my nightmare unfolds all around me. This is the basement I dreamed about. And this is where my body is leading me—closer to Maura, to what she's trying to tell me.

My mouth fills with a second helping of bile, causing my head to spin, for me to hunch forward and let it all out, my throat burning now. I wipe my mouth and take a few steps down the stairs. There's a thick steel door at the bottom, a giant letter M scribbled across it. I pull it open to allow myself through, holding its weight behind me so it doesn't slam shut.

A long, narrow hallway. I shine my light along the walls. Doors line both sides and overhead bulbs cast dim, yellowy light. I begin my way down, noting how the floors and walls are painted a deep green color, how the pipes leak overhead and make a pattering sound against the cement. How the lyrics to the "Miss Mary Mack" song have been scribbled on the walls along the way.

I take a deep breath, reminding myself that Maura wouldn't be leading me to any danger she didn't think I could handle. My stomach bubbles up again—like I'm getting closer. There's a knocking coming from the end of the hallway. I'm half-expecting it to be Maura, jumping rope. Even though I know she's dead.

I continue down the hallway, noticing the weathered, gray door at the very end—the one that faces me. The one from my nightmares. The knocking sound is coming from someplace around it, maybe from behind it.

"Hello, Stacey." It's Donovan's voice from the loudspeaker again. "Welcome back."

I bite down on my tongue to keep from crying out, and grip over my ears. But the knocking sound gets louder.

"I'm watching you," he says.

I'm shaking my head, trying to retain some sort of mindfulness. My stomach winces; bile squirts up toward my throat. I bend at the waist and dry heave—my stomach now completely empty.

I wipe my mouth with my sleeve, noticing how my cheeks are damp with tears. None of this makes sense. Maura is dead. Donovan is locked up. There's no way Cory and his group could have gotten him out. Plus, how is he related to my Maura nightmares? Why would he be waiting for me down here?

Unless someone told him—someone who knew all about my nightmares. Someone who could sense things about me that no one else knew.

"Stacey?" A voice from just behind me. Jacob's voice.

I turn around.

He emerges from the steel door, letting it slam shut behind him. "I knew I would find you here." He's pointing his flashlight beam right at me, so hard I have to block my eyes.

"Get away from me." I grip the crystal in my palm and ready myself to throw it.

"Stacey, you have to trust me." He takes a few steps closer. "Just listen to me for a second. I'm not going to hurt you."

"You heard me!" I shout.

Jacob ignores my warning and lunges right at me. He moves to grab the crystal, but I clench both hands around it and thrust with all my might up into his groin. Jacob buckles at the waist, but he doesn't go down.

I look at his feet . . . the rubber-soled sneakers. Just like the ones upstairs—the ones headed for the French room, for the séance. I take a step back and Jacob follows, still just inches from me. I swing toward his head but he catches the punch and grapples to restrain me. The storming in my stomach rages, inching up toward my throat again. I'm wasting time. I pull my neck back and plunge head-first into his forehead in a head-butt. Jacob staggers back, tripping over his feet. He falls, hitting his head against the cement wall.

I turn and run as fast as I can, down the hallway, where the knocking continues, becomes more urgent. I twist and pull at the doorknob with all my might, but it's no use. It just won't budge.

"Drea!" I shout into the door crack. "Is that you? Are you in there?" I pound and kick the door, jam my fingers into the crack until they bleed from splinters. Until I've exhausted myself completely. There's no more knocking. Just the pattering of water droplets against the floor. I scrunch down against the door and my throat fills with bile, causing me to choke, telling me that I can't give up, that I have to keep working.

I get up and try the knob again. Still locked. I take a deep breath and look around the framing of the door, noticing the ledge at the top. I reach up, run my finger along it, and feel a key. My hand shaking slightly, I stick the key in the hole and jiggle around until I hear the lock turn.

It's dark inside. I shine my flashlight around the perimeter of the room with one hand, and feel around the walls for a light switch with the other. My finger rubs over something sharp—a nail in the wall maybe.

I poke my bleeding finger into my mouth and look around the room. It's a small custodian's workroom—workbench to the right with tools scattered all over it, shelves loaded with paint cans, cleaning buckets, and rubber gloves, and a large buffer machine in the center. But what attracts me the most is the collection of origami; dozens of paper frogs, fish, birds, and more line the metal shelves.

My mouth turns dry and I heave, the breath catching in my throat, making me gag. A jump rope hangs from a hook at the back of the room. I move toward it and hear the door slam shut.

I let my eyes close and try to listen to my body and my intuition, not to think or reason or make sense out of all this. Not to fight it.

I know who it is. It's just like my mother and Jacob said—the truth lies in my past. And being here, in this shed—the familiar smell of mildew and must so thick in the air, the cracked cement walls—I feel like my past has been laid out all around me: Maura, having to vomit, the henna drawings, the forgotten promise. It's not about Cory and his gang, or Jacob, or even Drea. It's about stopping it from ever happening again. Stopping *him*. That's why I'm here. That's what Maura is trying to help me do.

He clicks the light switch on, and I turn around to find him. Miles Parker—the man who abducted Maura that day, who made her sick with his cherry brandy, drove drunk into a tree, and then carried her body off into the woods, leaving her in a tool shed until she died.

"That's the real thing, you know." He's pointing at the jump rope. "The actual rope she was jumping on the day I picked her up. Wanna touch it? Wanna see if it still smells like her?"

I clench my flashlight and feel my jaw lock.

"I'll never forget it," he continues. "She was jumping rope and singing that little song, the sidewalk around her all red from her crayon—from where she drew hearts and her favorite letter."

He smiles and I feel myself swallow, the inside of my mouth now a bit more moist, less dry and pasty.

Miles looks a lot different than the way he looked in court—older, scruffier, with sallow skin. His once sooty-dark hair has grayed quite a bit as well. It curls over his ears and hangs past the nape of his neck.

"I'm a little disappointed you didn't keep your promise," he says. "When you sent me that letter four years ago, I really expected you to follow through—to be waiting for my parole, to make me pay for what happened. Such an angry little girl." He's wearing a custodial uniform, like he planned this whole thing out—finding me, getting a job here.

"That was a long time ago," I say, noticing that he's also wearing a pair of work boots that have hard heels—the same boots that were no doubt following me from the dorm.

"Like yesterday to me," he snaps. "It's one of the things that kept me going. I wanted to meet the person who gave the police that anonymous tip."

"What are you talking about?" I take a step back, bumping into the buffer machine.

He smiles at me—his thin, chalky lips peeling back to reveal a chipped tooth in front. "The tip that led them to me. To the tool shed where the body was found. I've been waiting for this moment for a long time, Stacey Brown."

"I don't know what you're talking about," I say. "I didn't give any anonymous tip."

"Your letter said otherwise."

I think about it a moment, but it doesn't make sense. I didn't give any anonymous tip. I mean, I *should* have. I wanted to. But I didn't. The letter I sent him said I could only sense about the kidnapping, about where she was hidden. Any anonymous tip given to the police was from someone else.

"The letter didn't say that," I say. "It only said I had a *feeling* about Maura being taken, about where she was hidden."

"Why don't I believe you?"

I take another step back, bumping into a collection of mops, my spine pressed up against the cement wall now. "My friends are just upstairs," I say. "They're going to be wondering where I am."

"I know they're not your friends, Stacey. They're *my* friends. They've been helping me."

"What do you mean?" I feel my chin shake. I clench my teeth in an effort to halt the trembling.

"I've been watching you, Stacey," he pauses. "And I've been watching them. I know how interested they are in you. That gave us something in common, them and me. I thought getting a job here would be enough to get close to you. But, getting to know them . . . that was icing on the cake—made things so much easier."

"What are you talking about?"

"They told me about their plans for tonight, how they were going to get you here, how they wanted to try and recreate the scene from last year. They told me all about it, Stacey. You couldn't mind your own business then, either, could you?"

I swallow hard and try leaning back a little farther, as though the wall has the power to give way, but there isn't any room. I'm trapped.

"So what else could I do but help them?" he continues. "Give them access. I mean, here you are, just where I've wanted you. And all I had to do was give them a key."

"What do you want?"

"Payback," he says, taking another step, closing in on me. "You're a snake, Stacey. You should have minded your own business—should have kept your mouth shut. Do you have any idea what prison is like? What one has to do to occupy his time—to keep from going insane?"

I glance over his shoulder at the origami figures. Miles extends his hand to my chin to steal the glance back. I want to knock his hand away, but I don't. He towers over me; his weight is probably double mine.

My mind races with what I should do. Bite his hand? Try poking him in the eyes?

Miles reaches up to grab the jump rope. He drapes it around his shoulders and runs the handle along my cheek. "Don't worry," he says. "Ropes aren't my style. I prefer to use my hands. That gift I left you was just a little clue. Like the tape player and the letters—just little reminders. Could you sense that, too, Stacey—the way I've been watching you?"

"I didn't give any anonymous tip," I say, tears rolling down my cheeks. "You have to believe that it wasn't me." I glance to the left, spotting a hammer hanging on the wall. Miles drops the jump rope to the floor and places his thumbs at the front of my neck. "I don't like people who break their promises, Stacey. And I hate liars even more."

I clench my teeth, wondering how I can stall him, what I could possibly say to change his mind, get him to see the truth.

Miles dabs his fingers into my tears, a wide grin on his face, as though amused by my fear. I close my eyes a moment and concentrate on the crystal cluster rock in my pocket, on the sachet of thyme, conjuring up all the courage I have. And then I knee him—in the groin, as hard as I can. Miles staggers back a bit, enabling me to lunge for the hammer. My fingers just shy of the handle, he grabs my arm and spins me around, pushes my back up against the wall.

He pulls the hammer from its hook and presses it into my cheek. "Is this what you want?"

I shake my head and lock eyes with him. I need to be brave; I can't give up now. Just to my right, on the end of one of the shelves, is a fire extinguisher. Miles prods the hammer deeper into my cheek, forcing my bite to part. The inside of my cheek presses against the edges of my teeth— a burning, aching sensation.

"Feel good?" he asks.

I let out a cry.

Miles moves the hammer from my cheek and glances to the side to toss it. At the same moment I reach out, grab the extinguisher from the shelf. I knock it against his head—hard, a loud, cracking sound. Miles takes a couple steps back, moves his hands up toward his head. I aim the nozzle toward him and compress the handle. Nothing happens. Miles goes to grab the extinguisher from me. His fingers wrap around the base; mine are at the top, pulling at the thing with all my might. I feel my fingers slipping, losing grip.

Miles steps forward to gain a better position. That's when I spot the extinguisher's pin. I dive into the extinguisher, as though to tackle it, to pounce into the tug of war we've got going between us. I twist and go plummeting to the ground; my butt smacks against the cement flooring. But Miles' grip releases from the extinguisher. I aim it toward him, pull the pin, and compress the handle. A dark yellowish powder shoots out at him, sticks in his eyes.

I throw the extinguisher down and crawl toward the door. But he grips around my calf. I kick at his hand, plunge the heel of my shoe into his knuckles. Miles releases his grip and I go to reach up for the doorknob, but my fingers aren't quite long enough. I grapple up on my elbows to make it closer, but my fingers just graze the knob. Miles grabs at my ankle and drags me backward. I turn to face him. On his knees now, he holds the hammer high above his head. I hear myself scream. I scoot backward, away from him, but he just grabs at my ankle again and pulls me closer.

He's blinking his eyes from the extinguisher dust, like it's irritating him, settling into his eye sockets. I move slightly to the left, toward the buffer machine, wondering if I'd be able to push it at him, click it on with my foot, what that would do. That's when I spot the extinguisher, just inches from my leg.

The hammer still positioned high above his head, Miles seems almost wobbly on his knees. He moves his hand from my ankle and goes to rub at his eyes. I lean forward, grab the extinguisher and shoot it at him again—a strong and steady stream that knocks him backward.

I scoot back, reach up for the doorknob—this time able to grasp it—but I'm still too far away to turn the knob or push the door open. I look back at Miles, who has regained his balance. Back on his knees, he lunges toward me, swinging the hammer wildly. I plow to the right to avoid it. The hammer plunges into the door. I reach up for the knob again and turn and push. The door cracks open a couple inches. Miles grabs at my ankle to hold me in place just as the door whips open completely.

A pack of police officers bursts in. I feel myself being dragged up, moved to the side, out of the way. It's Jacob. I hesitate a moment, thinking how only minutes ago I had suspected him. He wraps his arms around me, and, instead of analyzing it, I just go with it. I allow myself to collapse into his embrace, trusting in my heart what I know is true.

"Are you okay?" he asks.

But I'm breathing so hard that I just can't answer.

A few moments later, the officers, including Mr. Abercrombie & Fitch, emerge from the custodial room with Miles in handcuffs. Miles looks in my direction but his eyes are so covered with dust, I'm not sure what he sees.

"It's over," Jacob says.

I press myself against him, like I never want to let go, hoping more than anything that he's right.

forty-five

It's busy in front of the O'Brian building when we get outside. Hanover police cruisers, campus administrators, and curious students collect about the place.

My mother is the first to emerge from the crowd of people. "Thank god you're okay," she says, wrapping her arms around me.

I hug her back with everything inside me. It feels so good to hold her this way, so long overdue. "How did you know I was here?"

"I just knew," she says, kissing the top of my head. She looks over my shoulder. "You must be Jacob."

Jacob takes a step forward to shake her hand.

"Thank you," she says, her eyes all black and runny from mascara.

"I didn't really do much," he says. "I wanted to do more."

"You did everything," she says. "You trusted your senses and you followed through on them. That's more than a lot of people would have done."

I hug my mother again, feeling completely restored by what she's saying, like maybe she's having second thoughts about using our senses to help others.

"I just hope someday you can forgive me for not helping you." My mother's once-tiny bird wings wrap around me, so much stronger than before.

I hug her even tighter, a trickle of tears sliding down the creases of my face, and tell her that I do forgive her.

"Hey, Mrs. B.," PJ says, interrupting us. He and Amber stand just behind us.

"Oh my god, how's Drea?" I ask.

"She's fine," Amber says. "A bit freaked, but fine."

"But you, on the other hand, Miss Drew . . ." PJ says. "Your phone messages scared the Crayola out of us."

"Thank you for calling the police," I say.

"*I* called them," my mother says. "I just had a feeling . . . an intuition."

"Well, thanks to all of you," I say.

"Are you kidding?" Amber says. "I should thank *you*. You scored me a date with one of Hillcrest's finest."

"What are you talking about?"

"Who else but that cutie-patootie police officer from the Hangman the other night."

Mr. Abercrombie & Fitch.

"Really, Amber," PJ says, "this trying-to-make-me-jealous routine is getting so old and pasty." He picks some of the yellow extinguisher dust from my shoulders and sprinkles it over his hair. "Cool color."

"You're such a freak show," Amber says to him.

"Correction," PJ says. "Freak show are those séance clonies. They got their sorry asses dragged out of here *tout de suite*. Not to mention immediate expulsion."

"And Donovan? Where is he?" I shiver just mentioning his name.

"Not here," PJ says. "Only his voice is. When the clonies got all groupie and went to visit him at the detention center, they recorded his voice and pieced it together to suit their twisted needs. Just ask Miss Donna Tillings over there; she's scooping it all to the police. When the clone-head ghost groupies got too freakish on her, she bailed on their plans. Maybe she isn't as dweeboid as I thought."

"Those guys deserve more than expulsion," Jacob says.

"So right you are, wise one," PJ says. "I'm just glad I was sensible enough not to let *my* bad ass get snagged up in their play."

"Oh, yeah, you're sensible," Amber says.

My mother stands beside me as I talk briefly to the police. It seems Cory and his group didn't even know I was in the building yet. They were waiting for me, getting all prepared for the séance and testing Donovan's tape over the loudspeaker until I arrived. It was Miles Parker following me to the O'Brian building from the dorm. Apparently, he's been working as a custodian here for a few weeks, which might explain how some of the windows and doors kept getting unlocked.

"But obviously Miles Parker wasn't involved in the séance or anything," I say. "He was just using Cory and them to get me here, right?"

The officer nods. "Just like they were using him for the key. Mr. Parker has no interest in contacting spirits."

"Just creating new ones," Amber says. She rests her chin on his perfectly bulgy arm and bats her fluorescent orange eyelashes up at him.

In the near distance, I spot Chad and Drea. They're sitting side by side on one of the benches, Chad's letterman jacket draped over Drea's shoulders—like an after-school special come to life. Exactly the way it should be.

Drea sees me as well. She gets up and comes and circles her arms around me. "I was so scared. Are you okay?"

"I will be," I say. "And you? Did they hurt you?"

She shakes her head. "I'm more embarrassed than anything. I was so totally stupid, Stacey." She proceeds to tell me how earlier tonight a teary-eyed Emma asked her to take a walk with her around campus. Between sobs and nose-blows, Emma told Drea that Cory had broken up with her tonight; she said she needed to get some air, couldn't bear to sit still in her room, and thought a little walk around campus might do her some good, take her mind off things. And even though Drea and Emma are hardly the best of friends or even friends for that matter, Drea felt bad for her and didn't want her to have to go alone. Only, once the two of them got near the O'Brian building, they *weren't* alone—Cory and Tobias appeared. They threatened Drea with pepper spray, dragged her into the building, and then locked her up in one of the classrooms.

"I just sort of freaked," Drea said. "And then, as soon as I heard Donovan's voice, I started going into panic attack mode; it was like last year all over again."

"I'm just glad you're okay," I say, hugging her once more.

"Thank you," she says. "You're always there when I need you."

"I'll always try to be."

I glance over at Chad. He's got his hands tucked deep in his pockets, making small talk with Jacob. He looks up at me at the same time. I move toward him and we just sort of stand there, staring at each other.

"You scared me," he says.

"Sorry," I say.

"No, I'm the one who's sorry," he says. "I should have believed you. I should have taken everything more seriously. I can be such an ass sometimes."

I shrug. "Maybe I should have done things differently too."

He takes me into his arms and kisses by my ear. "I love you, you know that? No matter what happens between us."

"No matter what happens?"

"Exactly," he says.

I nod and kiss his cheek, knowing full well what he means. "I love you, too," I say. And I mean it. I do love Chad. I love him enough to know that he and Drea belong together. "Friends?" I say.

"Always." He hugs me one last time before joining Drea back on the bench.

"So," my mother says, standing by my side again. She's shaking—a mix of fear and nervousness maybe—like I've never seen in her before. Her mouth is quivering and her eyes are completely filled. She sniffles a couple times to try and gain composure. "Shall we make some plans for to-morrow? I could call you—"

"You're crying," I say, noting how even the bravest of smiles cannot hide the way she really feels.

"I'm just so relieved that you're okay," she says, swiping at her tears. "And I'm so proud of you."

"Well, I'm pretty proud of you, too." I wrap my arms around her once more. "Thank you for everything."

"No," she says. "Thank *you*." She grips me extra tight. "I love you. I want you to know that."

"I do know it," I say. "And I love you, too."

"So sweet," Amber sings, interrupting us. "Like a Hall-mark card. When you care enough to squeeze the very best."

"Very cute," I say.

"Stace, you must be super-starving after upchucking so much chow this past week. So, does this mean you won't have to worry about any more heinous side effects?"

"For now, anyway."

"So how about we celebrate your barflessness with a little Denny's run. I could so go for a Lumberjack Slam."

"Is that supposed to sound appetizing?"

"You're welcome to come, too, Mrs. B," Amber adds.

"I'm a little tired," my mother says. "But thanks anyway." She waves goodbye before getting in her car and driving away.

"I'm tired, too," I say, peeking over at Jacob; he's waiting for me on the sidelines.

"Oh, yeah, I get it," Amber says, giving me an exaggerated wink. "Just do me a fave and hang a garter or something on the doorknob if you're a little *preoccupado*."

"A garter?"

She rolls her eyes. "Leave it to you to not own one stitch of chic. My dresser: top drawer on the left. But the leopard-print one with the tassels is totally off-limits."

"You're crazy," I say. "Jacob and I are just going to talk."

"Knowing you," she sighs, "you're probably right."

While Amber, PJ, Chad, and Drea head off to Denny's, I join Jacob on a walk back to the dorms. It's absolutely frigid and well past midnight. Jacob removes his coat and blankets it over my shoulders.

"I'm sorry I hit you," I say. "Are you okay?"

"I'll survive. I may never walk straight again, but at least I'll survive."

"I just wish I had trusted you."

"Well, I hope you can trust me now." He stops and I look up at him—into his pale blue eyes and at the strong set of his jaw—and feel my cheeks turn warm and pink.

"How did you know where to find me?" I ask.

"I just knew," he says, wiping a stray strand of hair from my face. "I dreamt it, remember?"

I swallow hard and look down, my palms all sweaty from nerves. "Why are we stopping?"

He nods toward my dorm. "Because we're here."

"Oh yeah," I say, just noticing it. "Well, thank you. For everything. Maybe you'll stick around. I mean, I know you've done what you came to do, and I know it must have been hard for you to just drop everything and move here. You must have a lot of friends back in Colorado."

Jacob smiles and takes a step closer, so close I can feel the warmth of his breath against my lips. "How could I leave?" he asks.

I look back up at him and my heart starts strumming inside my chest even harder than before. "I guess you can't."

We find ourselves back in my room, sitting on the floor with the chunky white candle my grandmother gave me between us. I unscrew the cap off my bottle of rose oil and pour a few droplets onto my fingers. The lush scent fills the air around us, reminding me of balmy beach nights, of hot passion fruit tea with dripping honey.

I sweep my oily fingers down the length of the candle to consecrate it. "As above," I say.

Jacob dabs his fingers with the oil and then runs them down the opposite side of the candle. "So below."

We continue taking turns, moistening around the circumference of the candle until it's fully anointed. Then I light a couple starter candles, one for each of us, and together Jacob and I use them to ignite the white candle.

"Blessed be," I say, looking up at Jacob as he extinguishes our starter candles with a snuffer.

"Blessed be," he repeats.

We sit there, our eyes locked on one another, for several seconds. I know in my heart we're both thinking the same thing. Jacob leans forward over the candle, the shadow of the flame dancing against his bottom lip. I lean forward to meet him as well. It's a kiss full of promise, of trust, and of all that is magic.

THE END

COMING IN
SEPTEMBER 2006

Homefree

NINA WRIGHT

Easter Hutton just might have the worst mom in the world. Does she really think her slime-ball boyfriend will divorce his wife just because Mom is pregnant? Missing her best friend and her dad, Easter just wants to blend in at her new school, which proves difficult when she starts experiencing involuntary bouts of astral-projection. She can't decide which is worse: these mysterious jaunts or the antics of her selfish, eccentric mother.

Everything changes when Easter discovers Homefree, an underground organization devoted to helping teenagers, like herself, with paranormal gifts. Suddenly she doesn't feel like an outsider anymore. Maybe a normal life—with real friends and a boyfriend—is possible after all.

0-7387-0927-1 / EAN 987-0-7387-0927-7

240 pages $8.95